The
Rancher

Center Point
Large Print

Also by Diana Palmer and available from
Center Point Large Print:

Maverick
Noelle
Diamond in the Rough
Will of Steel
True Blue

The
Rancher

DIANA
PALMER

CENTER POINT LARGE PRINT
THORNDIKE, MAINE

This Center Point Large Print edition is published
in the year 2013 by arrangement with
Harlequin Books S.A.

The text of this Large Print edition is unabridged.
In other aspects, this book may
vary from the original edition.
Printed in the United States of America
on permanent paper.
Set in 16-point Times New Roman type.

ISBN: 978-1-61173-596-3

Library of Congress Cataloging-in-Publication Data

Palmer, Diana.
The rancher / Diana Palmer. — Center Point Large Print edition.
pages cm
ISBN 978-1-61173-596-3 (library binding : alk. paper)
1. Ranches—Texas—Fiction. 2. Heirs—Fiction.
3. Bachelors—Fiction. 4. Neighbors—Fiction.
5. Large type books. I. Title.
PS3566.A513R36 2013
813'.54—dc23
                                          2012040113

The
Rancher

Dear Reader,

You probably think this book is about Cort Brannt, the brother of my heroine, Morie Brannt, in my mass-market Wyoming series called *Wyoming Tough*. Well, it's not. It's actually about the rooster who belongs to Cort's neighbor. A red rooster came into my yard several weeks ago. I tried to run him off, but he kept coming back. I discovered that roosters can fly, because he jumped a seven-foot high solid wooden fence to keep coming into my yard. I have lots of grass and a garden, which means bugs and worms and nice edibles. He wouldn't leave.

Over the weeks, people who work for me in the yard tried to catch him. Some of the neighbors got into the act. I especially wanted him gone because every time I went out to feed the birds or look at my garden, he would attack me. I was spurred three times, and I have the scars to prove it. So the rooster had to go. That presented a problem. I didn't want him killed or eaten, which left his fate up to me, since his owner apparently moved away and left him behind. (I don't blame him. If you knew this rooster, you wouldn't blame him, either!)

Our nice Mr. Martin, who looks after the koi and goldfish ponds for us, had a friend who knew how to catch chickens. He also kept chickens. So he just walked into the backyard, picked the rooster up and carried him off. My jaw is still dropping. Anyway, the rooster is very happy, has many hens to court, and I am happy because I can walk to my pumpkin patch without being mauled on the way.

Cort Brannt is going to have the same problem. His nice little frumpy neighbor has a pet rooster named Pumpkin and she loves him. She loves Cort, too, but Cort loves Odalie Everett who wants to train as a soprano and sing in the great opera houses of the world. Ah, the eternal triangle. It will all end well, I promise. And Pumpkin will have a happy future. Just like my unwanted red rooster visitor.

Hope you like the book. It has roots in Branntville, Texas, and spins off from one of my first romance novels, *To Love and Cherish*. King Brannt is Cort's dad.

Your greatest fan,

Diana Palmer

Chapter One

Maddie Lane was worried. She was standing in her big yard, looking at her chickens, and all she saw was a mixture of hens. There were red ones and white ones and gray speckled ones. But they were all hens. Someone was missing: her big Rhode Island Red rooster, Pumpkin.

She knew where he likely was. It made her grind her teeth together. There was going to be trouble, again, and she was going to be on the receiving end of it.

She pushed back her short, wavy blond hair and grimaced. Her wide gray eyes searched the yard, hoping against hope that she was mistaken, that Pumpkin had only gone in search of bugs, not cowboys.

"Pumpkin?" she called loudly.

Great-Aunt Sadie came to the door. She was slight and a little dumpy, with short, thin gray hair, wearing glasses and a worried look.

"I saw him go over toward the Brannt place, Maddie," she said as she moved out onto the porch. "I'm sorry."

Maddie groaned aloud. "I'll have to go after him. Cort will kill me!"

"Well, he hasn't so far," Sadie replied gently. "And he could have shot Pumpkin, but he didn't . . ."

"Only because he missed!" Maddie huffed. She sighed and put her hands on her slim hips. She had a boyish figure. She wasn't tall or short, just sort of in the middle. But she was graceful, for all that. And she could work on a ranch, which she did. Her father had taught her how to raise cattle, how to market them, how to plan and how to budget. Her little ranch wasn't anything big or special, but she made a little money. Things had been going fine until she decided she wanted to branch out her organic egg-laying business and bought Pumpkin after her other rooster was killed by a coyote, along with several hens. But now things weren't so great financially.

Maddie had worried about getting a new rooster. Her other one wasn't really vicious, but she did have to carry a tree branch around with her to keep from getting spurred. She didn't want another aggressive one.

"Oh, he's gentle as a lamb," the former owner assured her. "Great bloodlines, good breeder, you'll get along just fine with him!"

Sure, she thought when she put him in the chicken yard and his first act was to jump on her foreman, old Ben Harrison, when he started to gather eggs.

"Better get rid of him now," Ben had warned as

she doctored the cuts on his arms the rooster had made even through the fabric.

"He'll settle down, he's just excited about being in a new place," Maddie assured him.

Looking back at that conversation now, she laughed. Ben had been right. She should have sent the rooster back to the vendor in a shoebox. But she'd gotten attached to the feathered assassin. Sadly, Cort Brannt hadn't.

Cort Matthew Brannt was every woman's dream of the perfect man. He was tall, muscular without making it obvious, cultured, and he could play a guitar like a professional. He had jet-black hair with a slight wave, large dark brown eyes and a sensuous mouth that Maddie often dreamed of kissing.

The problem was that Cort was in love with their other neighbor, Odalie Everett. Odalie was the daughter of big-time rancher Cole Everett and his wife, Heather, who was a former singer and songwriter. She had two brothers, John and Tanner. John still lived at home, but Tanner lived in Europe. Nobody talked about him.

Odalie loved grand opera. She had her mother's clear, beautiful voice and she wanted to be a professional soprano. That meant specialized training.

Cort wanted to marry Odalie, who couldn't see him for dust. She'd gone off to Italy to study with some famous voice trainer. Cort was distraught and it didn't help that Maddie's rooster kept showing up in his yard and attacking him without warning.

"I can't understand why he wants to go all the way over there to attack Cort," Maddie said aloud. "I mean, we've got cowboys here!"

"Cort threw a rake at him the last time he came over here to look at one of your yearling bulls," Sadie reminded her.

"I throw things at him all the time," Maddie pointed out.

"Yes, but Cort chased him around the yard, picked him up by his feet, and carried him out to the hen yard to show him to the hens. Hurt his pride," Sadie continued. "He's getting even."

"You think so?"

"Roosters are unpredictable. That particular one," she added with a bite in her voice that was very out of character, "should have been chicken soup!"

"Great-Aunt Sadie!"

"Just telling you the way it is," Sadie huffed. "My brother—your granddaddy—would have killed him the first time he spurred you."

Maddie smiled. "I guess he would. I don't like killing things. Not even mean roosters."

"Cort would kill him for you if he could shoot straight," Sadie said with veiled contempt. "You load that .28 gauge shotgun in the closet for me, and I'll do it."

"Great-Aunt Sadie!"

She made a face. "Stupid thing. I wanted to pet the hens and he ran me all the way into the house. Pitiful, when a chicken can terrorize a whole ranch. You go ask Ben how he feels about that red rooster. I dare you. If you'd let him, he'd run a truck over it!"

Maddie sighed. "I guess Pumpkin is a terror. Well, maybe Cort will deal with him once and for all and I can go get us a nice rooster."

"In my experience, no such thing," the older woman said. "And about Cort dealing with him . . ." She nodded toward the highway.

Maddie grimaced. A big black ranch truck turned off the highway and came careening down the road toward the house. It was obviously being driven by a maniac.

The truck screeched to a stop at the front porch, sending chickens running for cover in the hen yard because of the noise.

"Great," Maddie muttered. "Now they'll stop laying for two days because he's terrified them!"

"Better worry about yourself," Great-Aunt Sadie said. "Hello, Cort! Nice to see you," she added with a wave and ran back into the house, almost at a run.

Maddie bit off what she was going to say about traitors. She braced herself as a tall, lean, furious cowboy in jeans, boots, a chambray shirt and a black Stetson cocked over one eye came straight

13

toward her. She knew what the set of that hat meant. He was out for blood.

"I'm sorry!" she said at once, raising her hands, palms out. "I'll do something about him, I promise!"

"Andy landed in a cow patty," he raged in his deep voice. "That's nothing compared to what happened to the others while we were chasing him. I went headfirst into the dipping tray!"

She wouldn't laugh, she wouldn't laugh, she wouldn't . . .

"Oh, hell, stop that!" he raged while she bent over double at the mental image of big, handsome Cort lying facedown in the stinky stuff they dipped cattle in to prevent disease.

"I'm sorry. Really!" She forced herself to stop laughing. She wiped her wet eyes and tried to look serious. "Go ahead, keep yelling at me. Really. It's okay."

"Your stupid rooster is going to feed my ranch hands if you don't keep him at home!" he said angrily.

"Oh, my, chance would be a fine thing, wouldn't it?" she asked wistfully. "I mean, I guess I could hire an off-duty army unit to come out here and spend the next week trying to run him down." She gave him a droll look. "If you and your men can't catch him, how do you expect me to catch him?"

"I caught him the first day he was here," he reminded her.

"Yes, but that was three months ago," she pointed out. "And he'd just arrived. Now he's learned evasion techniques." She frowned. "I wonder if they've ever thought of using roosters as attack animals for the military? I should suggest it to someone."

"I'd suggest you find some way to keep him at home before I resort to the courts."

"You'd sue me over a chicken?" she exclaimed. "Wow, what a headline that would be. Rich, Successful Rancher Sues Starving, Female Small-Rancher for Rooster Attack. Wouldn't your dad love reading that headline in the local paper?" she asked with a bland smile.

His expression was growing so hard that his high cheekbones stood out. "One more flying red feather attack and I'll risk it. I'm not kidding."

"Oh, me, neither." She crossed her heart. "I'll have the vet prescribe some tranquilizers for Pumpkin to calm him down," she said facetiously. She frowned. "Ever thought about asking your family doctor for some? You look very stressed."

"I'm stressed because your damned rooster keeps attacking me! On my own damned ranch!" he raged.

"Well, I can see that it's a stressful situation to be in," she sympathized. "With him attacking you, and all." She knew it would make him furious, but she had to know. "I hear Odalie Everett went to Italy."

The anger grew. Now it was cold and threatening. "Since when is Odalie of interest to you?"

"Just passing on the latest gossip." She peered at him through her lashes. "Maybe you should study opera . . ."

"You venomous little snake," he said furiously. "As if you could sing a note that wasn't flat!"

She colored. "I could sing if I wanted to!"

He looked her up and down. "Sure. And get suddenly beautiful with it?"

The color left her face.

"You're too thin, too flat-chested, too plain and too untalented to ever appeal to me, just in case you wondered," he added with unconcealed distaste.

She drew herself up to her full height, which only brought the top of her head to his chin, and stared at him with ragged dignity. "Thank you. I was wondering why men don't come around. It's nice to know the reason."

Her damaged pride hit him soundly, and he felt small. He shifted from one big booted foot to the other. "I didn't mean it like that," he said after a minute.

She turned away. She wasn't going to cry in front of him.

Her sudden vulnerability hurt him. He started after her. "Listen, Madeline," he began.

She whirled on her booted heel. Her pale eyes

shot fire at him. Her exquisite complexion went ruddy. Beside her thighs, her hands were clenched. "You think you're God's gift to women, don't you? Well, let me tell you a thing or two! You've traded on your good looks for years to get you what you want, but it didn't get you Odalie, did it?"

His face went stony. "Odalie is none of your damned business," he said in a soft, dangerous tone.

"Looks like she's none of yours, either," she said spitefully. "Or she'd never have left you."

He turned around and stomped back to his truck.

"And don't you dare roar out of my driveway and scare my hens again!"

He slammed the door, started the truck and deliberately gunned the engine as he roared out toward the main highway.

"Three days they won't lay, now," Maddie said to herself. She turned, miserable, and went up the porch steps. Her pride was never going to heal from that attack. She'd had secret feelings for Cort since she was sixteen. He'd never noticed her, of course, not even to tease her as men sometimes did. He simply ignored her existence most of the time, when her rooster wasn't attacking him. Now she knew why. Now she knew what he really thought of her.

Great-Aunt Sadie was waiting by the porch screen door. She was frowning. "No call for him to say that about you," she muttered. "Conceited man!"

Maddie fought tears and lost.

Great-Aunt Sadie wrapped her up tight and hugged her. "Don't you believe what he said. He was just mad and looking for a way to hurt you because you mentioned his precious Odalie. She's too good for any cowboy. At least, she thinks she is."

"She's beautiful and rich and talented. But so is Cort," Maddie choked out. "It really would have been a good match, to pair the Everetts' Big Spur ranch with Skylance, the Brannt ranch. What a merger that would be."

"Except that Odalie doesn't love Cort and she probably never will."

"She may come home with changed feelings," Maddie replied, drawing away. "She might have a change of heart. He's always been around, sending her flowers, calling her. All that romantic stuff. The sudden stop might open her eyes to what a catch he is."

"You either love somebody or you don't," the older woman said quietly.

"You think?"

"I'll make you a nice pound cake. That will cheer you up."

"Thanks. That's sweet of you." She wiped her eyes. "Well, at least I've lost all my illusions. Now I can just deal with my ranch and stop mooning over a man who thinks he's too good for me."

"No man is too good for you, sweetheart," Great-Aunt Sadie said gently. "You're pure gold. Don't you ever let anyone tell you different."

She smiled.

When she went out late in the afternoon to put her hens in their henhouse to protect them from overnight predators, Pumpkin was right where he should be—back in the yard.

"You're going to get me sued, you red-feathered problem child," she muttered. She was carrying a small tree branch and a metal garbage can lid as she herded her hens into the large chicken house. Pumpkin lowered his head and charged her, but he bounced off the lid.

"Get in there, you fowl assassin," she said, evading and turning on him.

He ran into the henhouse. She closed the door behind him and latched it, leaned back against it with a sigh.

"Need to get rid of that rooster, Miss Maddie," Ben murmured as he walked by. "Be delicious with some dumplings."

"I'm not eating Pumpkin!"

He shrugged. "That's okay. I'll eat him for you."

"I'm not feeding him to you, either, Ben."

He made a face and kept walking.

She went inside to wash her hands and put

antibiotic cream on the places where her knuckles were scraped from using the garbage can lid. She looked at her hands under the running water. They weren't elegant hands. They had short nails and they were functional, not pretty. She remembered Odalie Everett's long, beautiful white fingers on the keyboard at church, because Odalie could play as well as she sang. The woman was gorgeous, except for her snobbish attitude. No wonder Cort was in love with her.

Maddie looked in the mirror on the medicine cabinet above the sink and winced. She really was plain, she thought. Of course, she never used makeup or perfume, because she worked from dawn to dusk on the ranch. Not that makeup would make her beautiful, or give her bigger breasts or anything like that. She was basically just pleasant to look at, and Cort wanted beauty, brains and talent.

"I guess you'll end up an old spinster with a rooster who terrorizes the countryside."

The thought made her laugh. She thought of photographing Pumpkin and making a giant Wanted poster, with the legend, Wanted: Dead or Alive. She could hardly contain herself at the image that presented itself if she offered some outlandish reward. Men would wander the land with shotguns, looking for a small red rooster.

"Now you're getting silly," she told her image, and went back to work.

● ● ●

Cort Brannt slammed out of his pickup truck and into the ranch house, flushed with anger and self-contempt.

His mother, beautiful Shelby Brannt, glanced up as he passed the living room.

"Wow," she murmured. "Cloudy and looking like rain."

He paused and glanced at her. He grimaced, retraced his steps, tossed his hat onto the sofa and sat down beside her. "Yeah."

"That rooster again, huh?" she teased.

His dark eyes widened. "How did you guess?"

She tried to suppress laughter and lost. "Your father came in here bent over double, laughing his head off. He said half the cowboys were ready to load rifles and go rooster-hunting about the time you drove off. He wondered if we might need to find legal representation for you . . . ?"

"I didn't shoot her," he said. He shrugged his powerful shoulders and let out a long sigh, his hands dangling between his splayed legs as he stared at the carpet. "But I said some really terrible things to her."

Shelby put down the European fashion magazine she'd been reading. In her younger days, she had been a world-class model before she married King Brannt. "Want to talk about it, Matt?" she asked gently.

"Cort," he corrected with a grin.

21

She sighed. "Cort. Listen, your dad and I were calling you Matt until you were teenager, so it's hard . . ."

"Yes, well, you were calling Morie 'Dana,' too, weren't you?"

Shelby laughed. "It was an inside-joke. I'll tell it to you one day." She smiled. "Come on. Talk to me."

His mother could always take the weight off his shoulders. He'd never been able to speak so comfortably about personal things to his father, although he loved the older man dearly. He and his mother were on the same wavelength. She could almost read his mind.

"I was pretty mad," he confessed. "And she was cracking jokes about that stupid rooster. Then she made a crack about Odalie and I just, well, I just lost it."

Odalie, she knew, was a sore spot with her son. "I'm sorry about the way things worked out, Cort," she said gently. "But there's always hope. Never lose sight of that."

"I sent her roses. Serenaded her. Called her just to talk. Listened to her problems." He looked up. "None of that mattered. That Italian voice trainer gave her an invitation and she got on the next plane to Rome."

"She wants to sing. You know that. You've always known it. Her mother has the voice of an angel, too."

22

"Yes, but Heather never wanted fame. She wanted Cole Everett," he pointed out with a faint smile.

"That was one hard case of a man," Shelby pointed out. "Like your father." She shook her head. "We had a very, very rocky road to the altar. And so did Heather and Cole."

She continued pensively. "You and Odalie's brother, John Everett, were good friends for a while. What happened there?"

"His sister happened," Cort replied. "She got tired of having me at their place all the time playing video games with John and was very vocal about it, so he stopped inviting me over. I invited him here, but he got into rodeo and then I never saw him much. We're still friends, in spite of everything."

"He's a good fellow."

"Yeah."

Shelby got up, ruffled his hair and grinned. "You're a good fellow, too."

He laughed softly. "Thanks."

"Try not to dwell so much on things," she advised. "Sit back and just let life happen for a while. You're so intense, Cort. Like your dad," she said affectionately, her dark eyes soft on his face. "One day Odalie may discover that you're the sun in her sky and come home. But you have to let her try her wings. She's traveled, but only with her parents. This is her first real taste of freedom. Let her enjoy it."

"Even if she messes up her life with that Italian guy?"

"Even then. It's her life," she reminded him gently. "You don't like people telling you what to do, even if it's for your own good, right?"

He glowered at her. "If you're going to mention that time you told me not to climb up the barn roof and I didn't listen . . ."

"Your first broken arm," she recalled, and pursed her lips. "And I didn't even say I told you so," she reminded him.

"No. You didn't." He stared at his linked fingers. "Maddie Lane sets me off. But I should never have said she was ugly and no man would want her."

"You said that?" she exclaimed, wincing. "Cort . . . !"

"I know." He sighed. "Not my finest moment. She's not a bad person. It's just she gets these goofy notions about animals. That rooster is going to hurt somebody bad one day, maybe put an eye out, and she thinks it's funny."

"She doesn't realize he's dangerous," she replied.

"She doesn't want to realize it. She's in over her head with these expansion projects. Cage-free eggs. She hasn't got the capital to go into that sort of operation, and she's probably already breaking half a dozen laws by selling them to restaurants."

"She's hurting for money," Shelby reminded him somberly. "Most ranchers are, even us. The drought is killing us. But Maddie only has a few head of cattle and she can't buy feed for them if her corn crop dies. She'll have to sell at a loss. Her breeding program is already losing money." She shook her head. "Her father was a fine rancher. He taught your father things about breeding bulls. But Maddie just doesn't have the experience. She jumped in at the deep end when her father died, but it was by necessity, not choice. I'm sure she'd much rather be drawing pictures than trying to produce calves."

"Drawing." He said it with contempt.

She stared at him. "Cort, haven't you ever noticed that?" She indicated a beautiful rendering in pastels of a fairy in a patch of daisies in an exquisite frame on the wall.

He glanced at it. "Not bad. Didn't you get that at an art show last year?"

"I got it from Maddie last year. She drew it."

He frowned. He actually got up and went to look at the piece. "She drew that?" he asked.

"Yes. She was selling two pastel drawings at the art show. This was one of them. She sculpts, too—beautiful little fairies—but she doesn't like to show those to people. I told her she should draw professionally, perhaps in graphic design or even illustration. She laughed. She doesn't think she's good enough." She sighed. "Maddie is insecure.

She has one of the poorest self-images of anyone I know."

Cort knew that. His lips made a thin line. He felt even worse after what he'd said to her. "I should probably call and apologize," he murmured.

"That's not a bad idea, son," she agreed.

"And then I should drive over there, hide in the grass and shoot that damned red-feathered son of a . . . !"

"Cort!"

He let out a harsh breath. "Okay. I'll call her."

"Roosters don't live that long," she called after him. "He'll die of old age before too much longer."

"With my luck, he'll hit fifteen and keep going. Animals that nasty never die!" he called back.

He wanted to apologize to Maddie. But when he turned on his cell phone, he realized that he didn't even know her phone number. He tried to look it up on the internet, but couldn't find a listing.

He went back downstairs. His mother was in the kitchen.

"Do you know the Lanes' phone number?" he asked.

She blinked. "Well, no. I don't think I've ever tried to call them, not since Pierce Lane died last year, anyway."

"No number listed, anywhere," he said.

"You might drive by there later in the week," she suggested gently. "It's not that far."

He hesitated. "She'd lock the doors and hide inside when I drove up," he predicted.

His mother didn't know what to say. He was probably right.

"I need to get away," he said after a minute. "I'm wired like a piano. I need to get away from the rooster and Odalie and . . . everything."

"Why don't you go to Wyoming and visit your sister?" she suggested.

He sighed. "She's not expecting me until Thursday."

She laughed. "She won't care. Go early. It would do both of you good."

"It might at that."

"It won't take you long to fly up there," she added. "You can use the corporate jet. I'm sure your father wouldn't mind. He misses Morie. So do I."

"Yeah, I miss her, too," he said. He hugged his mother. "I'll go pack a bag. If that rooster shows up looking for me, put him on a plane to France, would you? I hear they love chicken over there. Get him a business-class ticket. If someone can ship a lobster from Maine," he added with a laugh, referring to a joke that had gone the rounds years before, "I can ship a chicken to France."

"I'll take it under advisement," she promised.

His mother was right, Cort thought that evening. He loved being with his sister. He and Morie were a lot alike, from their hot tempers to their very Puritan attitudes. They'd always been friends. When she was just five, she'd followed her big brother around everywhere, to the amusement of his friends. Cort was tolerant and he adored her. He never minded the kidding.

"I'm sorry about your rooster problems," Morie told him with a gentle laugh. "Believe me, we can understand. My poor sister-in-law has fits with ours."

"I like Bodie," he said, smiling. "Cane sure seems different these days."

"He is. He's back in therapy, he's stopped smashing bars and he seems to have settled down for good. Bodie's wonderful for him. She and Cane have had some problems, but they're mostly solved now," she said. She smiled secretly. "Actually, Bodie and I are going to have a lot more in common for the next few months."

Cort was quick. He glanced at her in the semidarkness of the front porch, with fireflies darting around. "A baby?"

She laughed with pure delight. "A baby," she said, and her voice was like velvet. "I only found out a little while ago. Bodie found out the day you showed up." She sighed. "So much happiness. It's almost too much to bear. Mal's over the moon."

"Is it a boy or a girl? Do you know yet?"

She shook her head. "Too early to tell. But we're not going to ask. We want it to be a surprise, however old-fashioned that might be."

He chuckled. "I'm going to be an uncle. Wow. That's super. Have you told Mom and Dad?"

"Not yet. I'll call Mom tonight, though."

"She'll be so excited. Her first grandchild."

Morie glanced at him. "You ever going to get married?" she asked.

"Sure, if Odalie ever says yes." He sighed. "She was warming up to me there just for a while. Then that Italian fellow came along and offered her voice training. He's something of a legend among opera stars. And that's what she wants, to sing at the Met." He grimaced. "Just my luck, to fall in love with a woman who only wants a career."

"I believe her mother was the same way, wasn't she?" Morie asked gently. "And then she and Cole Everett got really close. She gave up being a professional singer to come home and have kids. Although she still composes. That Wyoming group, Desperado, had a major hit from a song she wrote for them some years ago."

"I think she still composes. But she likes living on a ranch. Odalie hates it. She says she's never going to marry a man who smells like cow droppings." He looked at one of his big boots, where his ankle was resting on his other knee in

29

the rocking chair. "I'm a rancher, damn it," he muttered. "I can't learn another trade. Dad's counting on me to take over when he can't do the work anymore."

"Yes, I know," she said sadly. "What else could you do?"

"Teach, I guess," he replied. "I have a degree in animal husbandry." He made a face. "I'd rather be shot. I'd rather let that red-feathered assassin loose on my nose. I hate the whole idea of routine."

"Me, too," Morie confessed. "I love ranching. I guess the drought is giving Dad problems, too, huh?"

"It's been pretty bad," Cort agreed. "People in Oklahoma and the other plains states are having it worse, though. No rain. It's like the Dust Bowl in the thirties, people are saying. So many disaster declarations."

"How are you getting around it?"

"Wells, mostly," he said. "We've drilled new ones and filled the tanks to the top. Irrigating our grain crops. Of course, we'll still have to buy some feed through the winter. But we're in better shape than a lot of other cattle producers. Damn, I hate how it's going to impact small ranchers and farmers. Those huge combines will be standing in the shadows, just waiting to pounce when the foreclosures come."

"Family ranches are going to be obsolete one

day, like family farms," Morie said sadly. "Except, maybe, for the big ones, like ours."

"True words. People don't realize how critical this really is."

She reached over and squeezed his hand. "That's why we have the National Cattleman's Association and the state organizations," she reminded him. "Now stop worrying. We're going fishing tomorrow!"

"Really?" he asked, delighted. "Trout?"

"Yes. The water's just cold enough, still. When it heats up too much, you can't eat them." She sighed. "This may be the last chance we'll get for a while, if this heat doesn't relent."

"Tell me about it. We hardly had winter at all in Texas. Spring was like summer, and it's gone downhill since. I'd love to stand in a trout stream, even if I don't catch a thing."

"Me, too."

"Does Bodie fish?"

"You know, I've never asked. We'll do that tomorrow. For now," she said, rising, "I'm for bed." She paused and hugged him. "It's nice to have you here for a while."

"For me, too, little sis." He hugged her back, and kissed her forehead. "See you in the morning."

Chapter Two

Maddie hadn't thought about Cort for one whole hour. She laughed at herself while she fed her hens. Pumpkin was in the henhouse, locked in for the time being, so that she could feed the chickens without having to defend herself.

The laughter died away as she recalled the things Cort had said to her. She was ugly and flat-chested and he could never be attracted to her. She looked down at her slender body and frowned. She couldn't suddenly become beautiful. She didn't have the money to buy fancy clothes that flattered her, like Odalie did. In fact, her wardrobe was two years old.

When her father had been dying of cancer, every penny they had was tied up trying to keep up with doctor bills that the insurance didn't cover. Her father did carry life insurance, which was a lucky break because at his death, it was enough to pay back everybody.

But things were still hard. This year, they'd struggled to pay just the utility bills. It was going to come down to a hard choice, sell off cattle or sell off land. There was a developer who'd already been to see Maddie about selling the ranch. He wanted to build a huge hotel and amusement park complex. He was offering her over a million dollars, and he was persistent.

"You just run a few head of cattle here, don't you?" the tall man in the expensive suit said, but his smile didn't really reach his eyes. He was an opportunist, looking for a great deal. He thought Maddie would be a pushover once he pulled out a figure that would tempt a saint.

But Maddie's whole heritage was in that land. Her great-grandfather had started the ranch and suffered all sorts of deprivations to get it going. Her grandfather had taken over where he left off, improving both the cattle herd and the land. Her father had toiled for years to find just the right mix of grasses to pursue a purebred cattle breeding herd that was now the envy of several neighbors. All that would be gone. The cattle sold off, the productive grasslands torn up and paved for the complex, which would attract people passing by on the long, monotonous interstate highway that ran close to the border of the ranch.

"I'll have to think about it," she told him, nodding. Her smile didn't reach her eyes, either.

He pursed his lips. "You know, we're looking at other land in the area, too. You might get left out in the cold if we find someone who's more enthusiastic about the price we're offering."

Maddie didn't like threats. Even nice ones, that came with soft words and smiles.

"Whatever," she said. She smiled again. "I did say I'd have to think about it."

His smile faded, and his eyes narrowed. "You have a prime location here, only one close neighbor and a nearby interstate. I really want this place. I want it a lot."

"Listen, I hate being pressured . . . !"

He held up both hands. "Okay! But you think about it. You think hard." His expression became dangerous-looking. "We know how to deal with reluctant buyers. That's not a threat, it's just a statement. Here's my card."

She took it gingerly, as if she thought it had germs.

He made a huffing sound and climbed back into his fantastically expensive foreign car. He roared out of the driveway, scattering chickens.

She glared after it. No more eggs for two more days, she thought irritably. She'd rather starve than sell the ranch. But money was getting very tight. The drought was going to be a major hit to their poor finances, she thought dismally.

"Miss Maddie, you got that rooster locked up?" Ben called at the fence, interrupting her depressing reverie.

She turned. "Yes, Ben, he's restrained." She laughed.

"Thanks." He grimaced. "Going to feed the livestock and I'd just as soon not be mauled in the process."

"I know." She glanced at the wire door behind which Pumpkin was calling to the hens in that odd tone that roosters used when there was some special treat on the ground for them. It was actually a handful of mealworms that Maddie had tossed in the henhouse to keep him occupied while she locked him in.

Two of the hens went running to the door.

"He's lying," Maddie told them solemnly. "He's already eaten the mealworms, he just wants out."

"Cort left town, you hear?" Ben asked.

Her heart jumped. "Where did he go?" she asked miserably, waiting to hear that he'd flown to Italy to see Odalie.

"Wyoming, one of his cowboys said, to see his sister."

"Oh."

"Mooning over that Odalie girl, I guess," he muttered. "She said she hated men who smelled like cattle. I guess she hates her dad, then, because he made his fortune on the Big Spur raising cattle, and he still does!"

"She's just been spoiled," Maddie said quietly.

Ben glanced at her irritably. "She was mean to you when you were in school. Your dad actually went to the school to get it stopped. He went to see Cole Everett about it, too, didn't he?"

"Yes." She flushed. She didn't like remembering that situation, although Odalie had quickly stopped victimizing her after her father got involved.

"Had a nasty attitude, that one," Ben muttered. "Looked down her nose at every other girl and most of the boys. Thought she was too good to live in a hick town in Texas." His eyes narrowed. "She's going to come a cropper one day, you mark my words. What's that quote, 'pride goeth after a fall'? And she's got a lot farther to fall than some women."

"There's another quote, something about love your enemies?" she teased.

"Yes, well, she's given a lot of people reason to put that one into practice."

Maddie grimaced. "It must be nice, to have beauty and talent. I'd settle for one or the other myself." She laughed.

"You ought to be selling them little fairy statues you make," he advised. "Prettiest little things I ever saw. That one you sent my granddaughter for her birthday sits in the living room, because her mother loves to look at it. One of her friends has an art gallery in San Antonio. She said," he emphasized, "that you could make a fortune with those things."

Maddie flushed. "Wow."

"Not that those pretty drawings are bad, either. Sold one to Shelby Brannt, didn't you?"

"Yes." She'd loved the idea of Cort having to

36

see her artwork every day, because she knew that Shelby had mounted it on a wall in the dining room of her home. But he probably never even looked at it. Though cultured, Cort had little use for art or sculpture. Unless it was a sculpture of one of the ranch's prize bulls. They had one done in bronze. It sat on the mantel in the living room of the Brannt home.

"Ought to paint that rooster while he's still alive," Ben said darkly.

"Ben!"

He held up both hands. "Didn't say I was going to hurt him."

"Okay."

"But somebody else might." He pursed his lips. "You know, he could be the victim of a terrible traffic accident one day. He loves to run down that dirt road in front of the house."

"You bite your tongue," she admonished.

"Spoilsport."

"That visitor who came the other day, that developer, you see him again?" Ben asked curiously.

"No, but he left his name." She pulled his business card out of her pocket and held it up. "He's from Las Vegas. He wants to build a hotel and amusement park complex right here." She looked around wistfully. "Offered me a million dollars. Gosh, what I could do with that!"

"You could sell and throw away everything

your family worked for here?" Ben asked sadly. "My great-grandfather started working here with your great-grandfather. Our families have been together all that time." He sighed. "Guess I could learn to use a computer and make a killing with a dot-com business," he mused facetiously.

"Aw, Ben," she said gently. "I don't want to sell up. I was just thinking out loud." She smiled, and this time it was genuine. "I'd put a lot of people out of work, and God knows what I'd do with all the animals who live here."

"Especially them fancy breeding bulls and cows," he replied. "Cort Brannt would love to get his hands on them. He's always over here buying our calves."

"So he is."

Ben hesitated. "Heard something about that developer, that Archie Lawson fellow."

"You did? What?"

"Just gossip, mind."

"So? Tell me!" she prodded.

He made a face. "Well, he wanted a piece of land over around Cheyenne, on the interstate. The owner wouldn't sell. So cattle started dying of mysterious causes. So did the owner's dog, a big border collie he'd had for years. He hired a private investigator, and had the dog autopsied. It was poison. They could never prove it was Lawson, but they were pretty sure of it. See, he has a background in chemistry. Used to work at a big government lab, they say, before he started buying and selling land."

Her heart stopped. "Oh, dear." She bit her lip. "He said something about knowing how to force deals . . ."

"I'll get a couple of my pals to keep an eye on the cattle in the outer pastures," Ben said. "I'll tell them to shoot first and ask questions later if they see anybody prowling around here."

"Thanks, Ben," she said heavily. "Good heavens, as if we don't already have enough trouble here with no rain, for God knows how long."

"Everybody's praying for it." He cocked his head. "I know a Cheyenne medicine man. Been friends for a couple of years. They say he can make rain."

"Well!" She hesitated. "What does he charge?"

"He doesn't. He says he has these abilities that God gave him, and if he ever takes money for it, he'll lose it. Seems to believe it, and I hear he's made rain at least twice in the area. If things go from bad to worse, maybe we should talk to him."

She grinned. "Let's talk to him."

He chuckled. "I'll give him a call later."

Her eyebrows arched. "He has a telephone?"

"Miss Maddie," he scoffed, "do you think Native American people still live in teepees and wear headdresses?"

She flushed. "Of course not," she lied.

"He lives in a house just like ours, he wears jeans and T-shirts mostly and he's got a degree in anthropology. When he's not fossicking, they say he goes overseas with a group of mercs from Texas for top secret operations."

She was fascinated. "Really!"

"He's something of a local celebrity on the rez. He lives there."

"Could you call him and ask him to come over when he has time?"

He laughed. "I'll do that tonight."

"Even if he can't make rain, I'd love to meet him," she said. "He sounds very interesting."

"Take my word for it, he is. Doesn't talk much, but when he does, it's worth hearing. Well, I'll get back to work."

"Thanks, Ben."

He smiled. "My pleasure. And don't let that developer bully you," he said firmly. "Maybe you need to talk to Cort's dad and tell him what's going on. He's not going to like that, about the development. It's too close to his barns. In these hard times, even the Brannts couldn't afford to build new ones with all that high tech they use."

"Got a point. I'll talk to him."

Maddie went back to the house. She put the feed basket absently on the kitchen counter, mentally reviewing all the things she had planned for the week. She missed Cort already.

But at least it meant the rooster was likely to stay at home. He only went over to the Brannt ranch when Cort was in residence, to attack him.

"Better wash those eggs and put them in the refrigerator," Great-Aunt Sadie advised. "They're the ones for the restaurant, aren't they?"

"Yes. Old Mr. Bailey said his customers have been raving about the taste of his egg omelets lately." She laughed. "I'll have to give my girls a treat for that."

Great-Aunt Sadie was frowning. "Maddie, did you ever look up the law about selling raw products?"

Maddie shook her head. "I meant to. But I'm sure it's not illegal to sell eggs. My mother did it for years before she died. . . ."

"That was a long time ago, honey. Don't you remember that raid a few years ago on those poor farmers who were selling raw milk?" She made a face. "What sort of country do we live in? Sending an armed raid team after helpless farmers for selling milk!"

Maddie felt uneasy. "I'd forgotten that."

"I hadn't. In my day we had homemade butter and we could drink all the raw milk we wanted—didn't have all this fancy stuff a hundred years ago and it seems to me people were a whole lot healthier."

"You weren't here a hundred years ago," Maddie pointed out with a grin. "Anyway, the

41

government's not going to come out here and attack me for selling a few eggs!"

She did look on the internet for the law pertaining to egg production and found that she was in compliance. In fact, there were even places in the country licensed to sell raw milk. She'd have to tell Great-Aunt Sadie about that, she mused. Apparently armed teams weren't raiding farms out west.

Meanwhile, a day later, she did call King Brannt. She was hesitant about it. Not only was he Cort's father, he had a reputation in the county for being one tough customer, and difficult to get along with. He had a fiery temper that he wasn't shy about using. But the developer's determination to get the Lane ranch could have repercussions. A lot of them.

She picked up the phone and dialed the ranch.

The housekeeper answered.

"Could I speak to King Brannt, please?" she asked. "It's Maddie Lane."

There was a skirl of laughter. "Yes, you've got a rooster named Pumpkin."

Maddie laughed. "Is he famous?"

"He is around here," the woman said. "Cort isn't laughing, but the rest of us are. Imagine having a personal devil in the form of a little red rooster! We've been teasing Cort that he must have done something terrible that we don't know about."

Maddie sighed. "I'm afraid Pumpkin has it in for Cort. See, he picked him up by the feet and showed him to my girls, my hens, I mean, and hurt his pride. That was when he started looking for Cort."

"Oh, I see. It's vengeance." She laughed again. "Nice talking to you, I'll go get Mr. Brannt. Take just a minute . . ."

Maddie held on. Her gaze fell on one of her little fairy statues. It was delicate and beautiful; the tiny face perfect, lovely, with sculpted long blond hair, sitting on a stone with a butterfly in its hand. It was a new piece, one she'd just finished with the plastic sculpture mix that was the best on the market. Her egg money paid for the materials. She loved the little things and could never bear to sell one. But she did wonder if there was a market for such a specialized piece.

"Brannt," a deep voice said curtly.

She almost jumped. "Mr. Brannt? It's . . . I mean I'm Maddie Lane. I live on the little ranch next door to yours," she faltered.

"Hi, Maddie," he said, and his voice lost its curt edge and was pleasant. "What can I do for you?"

"I've got sort of a situation over here. I wanted to tell you about it."

"What's wrong? Can we help?"

"That's so nice of you." She didn't add that she'd been told some very scary things about his temper. "It's this developer. He's from Las Vegas . . ."

"Yes. Archie Lawson. I had him investigated."

"He's trying to get me to sell my ranch to him. I don't want to. This ranch has been in my family for generations. But he's very pushy and he made some threats."

"He's carried them out in the past," King said, very curtly. "But you can be sure I'm not going to let him hurt you or your cattle herd. I'll put on extra patrols on the land boundary we share, and station men at the cabin out there. We use it for roundup, but it's been vacant for a week or so. I'll make sure someone's there at all times, and we'll hook up cameras around your cattle herd and monitor them constantly."

"You'd do that for me?" she faltered. "Cameras. It's so expensive." She knew, because in desperation she'd looked at them and been shocked at the prices for even a cheap system.

"I'd do that for you," he replied. "You have one of the finest breeding herds I know of, which is why we buy so many of your young bulls."

"Why, thank you."

"You're welcome. You see, it's looking out for our interests as well as yours. I can't have a complex so close to my barns, or my purebred herd. The noise of construction would be bad enough, but the constant traffic would injure production."

"Yes, I know what you mean."

"Besides that, Lawson is unscrupulous. He's got his fingers in lots of dirty pies. He's had several brushes with the law, too."

"I'm not surprised. He was a little scary."

"Don't you worry. If he comes back and makes any threat at all, you call over here. If you can't find me, talk to Cort. He'll take care of it."

She hesitated. "Actually Cort isn't speaking to me right now."

There was a pause. "Because of the rooster?" His voice was almost smiling.

"Actually because I made a nasty crack about Odalie Everett," she confessed heavily. "I didn't mean to. He made me mad. I guess he was justified to complain. Pumpkin is really mean to him."

"So I heard. That rooster has had brushes with several of our cowboys." She could tell that he was trying not to laugh.

"The man who sold him to me said he was real gentle and wouldn't hurt a fly. That's sort of true. I've never seen Pumpkin hurt a fly." She laughed. "Just people."

"You need a gentle rooster, especially if you're going to be selling eggs and baby chicks."

"The baby chick operation is down the road, but I'm doing well with my egg business."

"Glad to hear it. Our housekeeper wants to get on your customer list, by the way."

"I'll talk to her, and thanks!"

He chuckled. "My pleasure."

"If Mr. Lawson comes back, I'll let you know."

"Please do. The man is trouble."

"I know. Thanks again, Mr. Brannt. I feel better now."

"Your dad was a friend of mine," he said quietly. "I miss him. I know you do, too."

"I miss him a lot," she said. "But Great-Aunt Sadie and I are coping. It's just this ranching thing," she added miserably. "Dad was good at it, he had charts in the barn, he knew which traits to breed for, all that technical stuff. He taught me well, but I'm not as good as he was at it. Not at all. I like to paint and sculpt." She hesitated. "Creative people shouldn't have to breed cattle!" she burst out.

He laughed. "I hear you. Listen, suppose I send Cort over there to help you with the genetics? He's even better at it than I am. And I'm good. No conceit, just fact."

She laughed, too. "You really are. We read about your bulls in the cattle journals." She paused. "I don't think Cort would come."

"He'll come." He sounded certain of it. "He needs something to take his mind off that woman. She's a sweet girl, in her way, but she's got some serious growing up to do. She thinks the world revolves around her. It doesn't."

"She's just been a little spoiled, I think." She tried to be gracious.

"Rotten," he replied. "My kids never were."

"You and Mrs. Brannt did a great job with yours. And John Everett is a really nice man. So the Everetts did a great job there, too." She didn't mention the second Everett son, Tanner. The Everetts never spoke about him. Neither did anyone else. He was something of a mystery man. But gossip was that he and his dad didn't get along.

"They did a great job on John, for sure." He let out a breath. "I just wish Cort would wake up. Odalie is never going to settle in a small community. She's meant for high society and big cities. Cort would die in a high-rise apartment. He's got too much country in him, although he'd jump at the chance if Odalie would offer him one. Just between us," he added quietly, "I hope she doesn't. If she makes it in opera, and I think she can, what would Cort do with himself while she trained and performed? He'd be bored out of his mind. He doesn't even like opera. He likes country-western."

"He plays it very well," Maddie said softly. "I loved coming to the barbecue at your place during the spring sale and hearing him sing. It was nice of you to invite all of us. Even old Ben. He was over the moon."

He laughed. "You're all neighbors. I know you think of Ben as more family than employee. His family has worked for your family for four generations."

"That's a long time," she agreed. "I'm not selling my place," she added firmly. "No matter what that fancy Las Vegas man does."

"Good for you. I'll help you make sure of that. I'll send Cort on over."

"He's back from visiting his sister?" she stammered.

"Yes. Got back yesterday. They went trout fishing."

She sighed. "I'd love to go trout fishing."

"Cort loves it. He said they did close the trout streams for fishing a couple of days after he and Dana—Morie, I mean, went. The heat makes it impossible."

"That's true." She hesitated. "Why do you call Morie Dana?" she blurted out.

He laughed. "When Shelby was carrying them, we called them Matt and Dana. Those were the names we picked out. Except that two of our friends used those names for theirs and we had to change ours. It got to be a habit, though, until the kids were adolescents.

"Hey, Cort," she heard King call, his hand covering the receiver so his voice was a little muffled.

"Yes, Dad?" came the reply.

"I want you to go over to the Lane place and give Maddie some help with her breeding program."

"The hell I will!" Cort burst out.

The hand over the phone seemed to close, because the rest of it was muffled. Angry voices, followed by more discussion, followed like what seemed a string of horrible curses from Cort.

King came back on the line. "He said he'd be pleased to come over and help," he lied. "But he did ask if you'd shut your rooster up first." He chuckled.

"I'll put him in the chicken house right now." She tried not to sound as miserable as she felt. She knew Cort didn't want to help her. He hated her. "And thank you again."

"You're very welcome. Call us if you need help with Lawson. Okay?"

"Okay."

True to his father's words, Cort drove up in front of the house less than an hour later. He wasn't slamming doors or scattering chickens this time, either. He looked almost pleasant. Apparently his father had talked to him very firmly.

Maddie had combed her hair and washed her face. She still wasn't going to win any beauty contests. She had on her nicest jeans and a pink T-shirt that said La Vie en Rose.

It called attention, unfortunately, to breasts that were small and pert instead of big and tempting. But Cort was looking at her shirt with his lips pursed.

"The world through rose-colored glasses?" he mused.

"You speak French."

"Of course. French, Spanish and enough German to get me arrested in Munich. We do cattle deals all over the world," he added.

"Yes, I remember." She swallowed, hard, recalling the things he'd said at their last unfortunate meeting. "Your father said you could help me figure out Dad's breeding program."

"I think so. I helped him work up the new one before he passed away," he added quietly. "We were all shocked by how fast it happened."

"So were we," Maddie confessed. "Two months from the time he was diagnosed until he passed on." She drew in a long breath. "He hated tests, you know. He wouldn't go to the doctor about anything unless he was already at death's door. I think the doctor suspected something, but Dad just passed right over the lecture about tests being necessary and walked out. By the time they diagnosed the cancer, it was too late for anything except radiation. And somebody said that they only did that to help contain the pain." Her pale eyes grew sad. "It was terrible, the pain. At the last, he was so sedated that he hardly knew me. It was the only way he could cope."

"I'm sorry," he said. "I haven't lost parents, but I lost both my grandparents. They were wonderful people. It was hard to let them go."

"Life goes on," she said quietly. "Everybody dies. It's just a matter of how and when."

"True."

She swallowed. "Dad kept his chalkboard in the barn, and his books in the library, along with his journals. I've read them all, but I can't make sense of what he was doing. I'm not college educated, and I don't really know much about animal husbandry. I know what I do from watching Dad."

"I can explain it to you."

She nodded. "Thanks."

She turned and led the way to the house.

"Where's that . . . rooster?" he asked.

"Shut up in the henhouse with a fan."

"A fan?" he exclaimed and burst out laughing.

"It really isn't funny," she said softly. "I lost two of my girls to the heat. Found them dead in the henhouse, trying to lay. I had Ben go and get us a fan and install it there. It does help with the heat, a little at least."

"My grandmother used to keep hens," he recalled. "But we only have one or two now. Foxes got the rest." He glanced at her. "Andie, our housekeeper, wants to get on your egg customer list for two dozen a week."

She nodded. "Your dad mentioned that. I can do that. I've got pullets that should start laying soon. My flock is growing by leaps and bounds." She indicated the large fenced chicken yard, dotted with all sorts of chickens. The henhouse was huge, enough to accommodate them all, complete with perches and ladders and egg boxes and, now, a fan.

"Nice operation."

"I'm going to expand it next year, if I do enough business."

"Did you check the law on egg production?"

She laughed. "Yes, I did. I'm in compliance. I don't have a middleman, or I could be in trouble. I sell directly to the customer, so it's all okay."

"Good." He shrugged, his hands in his jean pockets. "I'd hate to have to bail you out of jail."

"You wouldn't," she sighed.

He stopped and looked down at her. She seemed so dejected. "Yes, I would," he said, his deep voice quiet and almost tender as he studied her small frame, her short wavy blond hair, her wide, soft gray eyes. Her complexion was exquisite, not a blemish on it except for one small mole on her cheek. She had a pretty mouth, too. It looked tempting. Bow-shaped, soft, naturally pink . . .

"Cort?" she asked suddenly, her whole body tingling, her heart racing at the way he was staring at her mouth.

"What? Oh. Yes. The breeding books." He nodded. "We should get to it."

"Yes." She swallowed, tried to hide her blush and opened the front door.

Chapter Three

Maddie couldn't help but stare at Cort as he leaned over the desk to read the last page of her father's breeding journal. He was the handsomest man she'd ever seen. And that physique! He was long and lean, but also muscular. Broad-shouldered, narrow-hipped, and in the opening of his chambray shirt, thick curling black hair peeked out.

She'd never been overly interested in intimacy. Never having indulged, she had no idea how it felt, although she'd been reading romance novels since her early teens. She did know how things worked between men and women from health class. What she didn't know was why women gave in to men. She supposed it came naturally.

Cort felt her eyes on him and turned, so that he was looking directly into her wide, shocked gray eyes. His own dark ones narrowed. He knew that look, that expression. She was trying to hide it, but he wasn't fooled.

"Take a picture," he drawled, because her interest irritated him. She wasn't his type. Not at all.

Her reaction shamed him. She looked away,

cleared her throat and went beet-red. "Sorry," she choked. "I was just thinking. You were sort of in the way. I was thinking about my fairies . . ."

He felt guilty. That made him even more irritable. "What fairies?"

She stumbled and had to catch herself as she went past him. She was so embarrassed she could hardly even walk.

She went to the shelf where she'd put the newest one. Taking it down very carefully, she carried it to the desk and put it in front of him.

He caught his breath. He picked it up, delicately for a man with such large, strong hands, and held it up to his eyes. He turned it. He was smiling. "This is really beautiful," he said, as if it surprised him. He glanced at her. "You did this by yourself?"

She moved uneasily. "Yes," she muttered. What did he think—that she had somebody come in and do the work so she could claim credit for it?

"I didn't mean it like that, Maddie," he said gently. The sound of her name on his lips made her tingle. She didn't dare look up, because her attraction to him would surely show. He knew a lot more about women than she knew about men. He could probably tell already that she liked him. It had made him mad. So she'd have to hide it.

"Okay," she said. But she still wouldn't look up.

He gave the beautiful little statuette another look before he put it down very gently on the desk. "You should be marketing those," he said firmly. "I've seen things half as lovely sell for thousands of dollars."

"Thousands?" she exclaimed.

"Yes. Sometimes five figures. I was staying at a hotel in Arizona during a cattlemen's conference and a doll show was exhibiting at the same hotel. I talked to some of the artists." He shook his head. "It's amazing how much collectors will pay for stuff like that." He indicated the fairy with his head. "You should look into it."

She was stunned. "I never dreamed people would pay so much for a little sculpture."

"Your paintings are nice, too," he admitted. "My mother loves the drawing you did. She bought it at that art show last year. She said you should be selling the sculptures, too."

"I would. It's just that they're like my children," she confessed, and flushed because that sounded nutty. "I mean . . . well, it's hard to explain."

"Each one is unique and you put a lot of yourself into it," he guessed. "So it would be hard to sell one."

"Yes." She did look up then, surprised that he was so perceptive.

"You have the talent. All you need is the drive."

"Drive." She sighed. She smiled faintly. "How about imminent starvation? Does that work for drive?"

He laughed. "We wouldn't let you starve. Your

bull calves are too valuable to us," he added, just when she thought he might actually care.

"Thanks," she said shyly. "In that journal of Dad's—" she changed the subject "—he talks about heritability traits for lean meat with marbling to produce cuts that health-conscious consumers will buy. Can you explain to me how I go about producing herd sires that carry the traits we breed for?"

He smiled. "It's complicated. Want to take notes?"

She sighed. "Just like going back to school." Then she remembered school, and the agonies she went through in her junior and senior years because of Odalie Everett, and her face clenched.

"What's wrong?" he asked, frowning.

She swallowed. She almost said what was wrong. But she'd been down that road with him already, making comments she shouldn't have made about Odalie. She wasn't going to make him mad. Not now, when he was being pleasant and helpful.

"Nothing. Just a stray thought." She smiled. "I'll get some paper and a pencil."

After a half hour she put down the pencil. "It's got to be like learning to speak Martian," she muttered.

He laughed out loud. "Listen, I didn't come into the world knowing how this stuff worked, either.

I had to learn it, and if my dad hadn't been a patient man, I'd have jumped off a cliff."

"Your dad is patient?" she asked, and couldn't help sounding surprised.

"I know he's got a reputation for being just the opposite. But he really is patient. I had a hard time with algebra in high school. He'd take me into the office every night and go over problems with me until I understood how to do them. He never fussed, or yelled, or raised his voice. And I was a problem child." He shook his head. "I'm amazed I got through my childhood in one piece. I've broken half the bones in my body at some point, and I know my mother's gray hairs are all because of me. Morie was a little lady. She never caused anybody any trouble."

"I remember," Maddie said with a smile. "She was always kind to me. She was a couple of years ahead of me, but she was never snobby."

His dark eyes narrowed. "There's a hidden comment in there."

She flushed. "I didn't mention anybody else."

"You meant Odalie," he said. "She can't help being beautiful and rich and talented," he pointed out. "And it wasn't her fault that her parents put her in public school instead of private school, where she might have been better treated."

"Better treated." She glared at him. "Not one teacher or administrator ever had a bad word to say about her, even though she bullied younger girls mercilessly and spent most of her time bad-mouthing people she didn't like. One year she had a party for our whole class, at the ranch. She invited every single girl in the class—except me."

Cort's eyes narrowed. "I'm sure it wasn't intentional."

"My father went to see her father, that's how unintentional it was," she replied quietly. "When Cole Everett knew what she'd done to me, he grounded her for a month and took away her end-of-school trip as punishment."

"That seems extreme for not inviting someone to a party," he scoffed.

"I guess that's because you don't know about the other things she did to me," she replied.

"Let me guess—she didn't send you a Valentine's Day card, either," he drawled in a tone that dripped sarcasm.

She looked at him with open sadness. "Sure. That's it. I held a grudge because she didn't send me a holiday card and my father went to see the school principal and Odalie's father because he liked starting trouble."

Cort remembered her father. He was the mildest, most forgiving man anywhere around Branntville. He'd walk away from a fight if he could. The very fact that he got involved meant that he felt there was more than a slight problem.

But Cort loved Odalie, and here was this bad-tempered little frump making cracks about her, probably because she was jealous.

"I guess if you don't have a real talent and you aren't as pretty, it's hard to get along with someone who has it all," he commented.

Her face went beet-red. She stood up, took her father's journal, closed it and put it back in the desk drawer. She faced him across the width of the desk.

"Thank you for explaining the journal to me," she said in a formal tone. "I'll study the notes I took very carefully."

"Fine." He started to leave, hesitated. He turned and looked back at her. He could see an unusual brightness in her eyes. "Look, I didn't mean to hurt your feelings. It's just, well, you don't know Odalie. She's sweet and kind, she'd never hurt anybody on purpose."

"I don't have any talent, I'm ugly and I lie." She nodded. "Thanks."

"Hell, I never said you lied!"

She swallowed. Loud voices and curses made her nervous. She gripped the edge of the desk.

"Now what's wrong?" he asked angrily.

She shook her head. "Nothing," she said quickly.

He took a sudden, quick step toward her. She backed up, knocked over the desk chair and almost fell again getting it between him and herself. She was white in the face.

He stopped in his tracks. His lips fell open. In

all his life, he'd never seen a woman react that way.

"What the hell is wrong with you?" he asked, but not in a loud or menacing tone.

She swallowed. "Nothing. Thanks for coming over."

He scowled. She looked scared to death.

Great-Aunt Sadie had heard a crash in the room. She opened the door gingerly and looked in. She glanced from Maddie's white face to Cort's drawn one. "Maddie, you okay?" she asked hesitantly, her eyes flicking back and forth to Cort's as if she, too, was uneasy.

"I'm fine. I just . . . knocked the chair over." She laughed, but it was a nervous, quick laugh. "Cort was just leaving. He gave me lots of information."

"Nice of him," Sadie agreed. She moved closer to Maddie, as if prepared to act as a human shield if Cort took another step toward the younger woman. "Good night, Cort."

He wanted to know what was wrong. It was true he'd said some mean things, but the fear in Maddie's eyes, and the looks he was getting, really disturbed him. He moved to the door, hesitated. "If you need any more help . . ." he began.

"I'll call. Sure. Thanks for offering." Maddie's voice sounded tight. She was standing very still. He was reminded forcibly of deer's eyes in headlights.

"Well, I'll get on home. Good night."

"Night," Maddie choked out.

He glanced from one woman to the other, turned and pulled the door closed behind him.

Maddie almost collapsed into the chair. Tears were running down her cheeks. Great-Aunt Sadie knelt beside the chair and pulled her close, rocking her. "There, there, it's all right. He's gone. What happened?"

"I mentioned about Odalie not inviting me to the party and he said I was just jealous of her. I said something, I don't . . . remember what, and he started toward me, all mad and impatient . . ." She closed her eyes, shivering. "I can't forget. All those years ago, and I still can't forget!"

"Nobody ever told Cort just what Odalie did to you, did they?"

"Apparently not," Maddie said heavily. She wiped her eyes. "Her dad made her apologize, but I know she never regretted it." She drew in a breath. "I told her that one day somebody was going to pay her back for all the mean things she did." She looked up. "Cort thinks she's a saint. If he only knew what she's really like . . ."

"It wouldn't matter," the older woman said sadly. "Men get hooked on a pretty face and they'd believe white was black if the woman told them it was. He's infatuated, baby. No cure for that but time."

"I thought he was so sexy." Maddie laughed.

She brushed at her eyes again. "Then he lost his temper like that. He scared me," she said on a nervous smile.

"It's all right. Nobody's going to hurt you here. I promise."

She hugged the older woman tight. "Thanks."

"At the time, that boy did apologize, and he meant it," Sadie reminded her. "He was as much a victim as you were."

"Yes, but he got in trouble and he should have. No man, even an angry young one with justification, should ever do what he did to a girl. He didn't have nightmares for a month, either, did he, or carry emotional scars that never go away? Sad thing about him," she added quietly, "he died overseas when a roadside bomb blew up when he was serving in the Middle East. With a temper like that, I often wondered what he might do to a woman if he got even more upset than he was at me that time."

"No telling. And just as well we don't have to find out." Her face hardened. "But you're right about that Odalie girl. Got a bad attitude and no compassion for anybody. One of these days, life is going to pay her out in her own coin. She'll be sorry for the things she's done, but it will be too late. God forgives," she added. "But there's a price."

"What's that old saying, 'God's mill grinds slowly, but relentlessly'?"

"Something like that. Come on. I'll make you a nice cup of hot coffee."

"Make that a nice cup of hot chocolate instead," Maddie said. "I've had a rough day and I want to go to bed."

"I don't blame you. Not one bit."

Cort was thoughtful at breakfast the next morning. He was usually animated with his parents while he ate. But now he was quiet and retrospective.

"Something wrong?" his dad asked.

Cort glanced at him. He managed a smile. "Yeah. Something." He sipped coffee. "I went over her dad's journal with Maddie. We had sort of an argument and I started toward her while I was mad." He hesitated. "She knocked over a chair getting away from me. White in the face, shaking all over. It was an extreme reaction. We've argued before, but that's the first time she's been afraid of me."

"And you don't understand why." His father's expression was troubled.

"I don't." Cort's eyes narrowed. "But you do, don't you?"

He nodded.

"King, should you tell him?" Shelby asked worriedly.

"I think I should, honey," he said gently, and his dark eyes smiled with affection. "Somebody needs to."

"Okay then." She got up with her coffee. "You men talk. I'm going to phone Morie and see how she's doing."

"Give her my love," King called after her.

"Mine, too," Cort added.

She waved a hand and closed the door behind her. "Tell me," Cort asked his dad.

King put down his coffee cup. "In her senior year, Maddie was Odalie's worst enemy. There was a boy, seemingly a nice boy, who liked Maddie. But Odalie liked him, and she was angry that Maddie, a younger girl who wasn't pretty or rich or talented, seemed to be winning in the affection sweepstakes."

"I told Maddie, Odalie's not like that," Cort began angrily.

King held up a hand. "Just hear me out. Don't interrupt."

Cort made a face, but he shut up.

"So Odalie and a girlfriend got on one of the social websites and started posting things that she said Maddie told her about the boy. She said Maddie thought he was a hick, that his mother was stupid, that both his parents couldn't even pass a basic IQ test."

"What? That's a lie . . . !"

"Sit down!" King's voice was soft, but the look in his eyes wasn't. Cort sat.

"The boy's mother was dying of cancer. He was outraged and furious at what Maddie had allegedly said about his family. His mother had just been taken to the hospital, not expected to live. She died that same day. He went to school just to find Maddie. She was in the library." He picked up his cup and sipped coffee. "He jerked her out of her chair, slapped her over a table and pulled her by her hair to the window. He was in the act of throwing her out—and it was on the second floor—when the librarian screamed for help and two big, stronger boys restrained him, in the nick of time."

Cort's face froze. "Maddie told you that?"

"Her father's lawyer told Cole Everett that," came the terse reply. "There were at least five witnesses. The boy was arrested for assault. It was hushed up, because that's what's done in small communities to protect the families. Odalie was implicated, because the attorney hired a private investigator to find the source of the allegations. They traced the posts to her computer."

Cort felt uneasy. He was certain Odalie couldn't have done such a thing. "Maybe somebody used her computer," he began.

"She confessed," King said curtly.

Cort was even more uneasy now.

"Cole Everett had his own attorney speak to the one Maddie's father had hired. They worked out a compromise that wouldn't involve a trial. But Odalie had to toe the line from that time forward. They put her on probation, you see. She had first-offender status, so her record was wiped when she stayed out of trouble for the next two years. She had a girlfriend who'd egged her on. The girl-friend left town shortly thereafter."

"Yes," Cort replied, relaxing. "I see now. The girlfriend forced her to do it."

King made a curt sound deep in his throat. "Son, nobody forced her to do a damned thing. She was jealous of Maddie. She was lucky the boy didn't kill Maddie, or she'd have been an accessory to murder." He watched Cort's face pale. "That's right. And I don't think even Cole Everett could have kept her out of jail if that had happened."

Cort leaned back in his chair. "Poor Odalie."

"Funny," King said. "I would have said, 'Poor Maddie.' "

Cort flushed. "It must have been terrible for both of them, I suppose."

King just shook his head. He got up. "Blind as a bat," he mused. "Just like me, when I was giving your mother hell twice a day for being engaged to my little brother. God, I hated him. Hated them both. Never would admit why."

"Uncle Danny?" Cort exclaimed. "He was engaged to Mom?"

"He was. It was a fake engagement, however." He chuckled. "He was just trying to show me what my feelings for Shelby really were. I forgave him every minute's agony. She's the best thing that ever happened to me. I didn't realize how deeply a man could love a woman. All these years," he added in a soft tone, "and those feelings haven't lessened a bit. I hope you find that sort of happi-ness in your life. I wish it for you."

"Thanks," Cort said. He smiled. "If I can get Odalie to marry me, I promise you, I'll have it."

King started to speak, but thought better of it. "I've got some book work to do."

"I've got a new video game I'm dying to try." Cort chuckled. "It's been a long day."

"I appreciate you going over to talk to Maddie."

"No problem. She just needed a few pointers."

"She's no cattlewoman," King said worriedly. "She's swimming upstream. She doesn't even like cattle. She likes chickens."

"Don't say chickens," Cort pleaded with a groan.

"Your problem isn't with chickens, it's with a rooster."

"I'd dearly love to help him have a fatal heart attack," Cort said irritably.

"He'll die of old age one day." His dad laughed.

"Maddie said that developer had been putting pressure on her to sell," King added solemnly. "I've put on some extra help to keep an eye over that way, just to make sure her breeding stock doesn't start dying mysteriously."

"What?" Cort asked, shocked. "She didn't say anything about that."

"Probably wouldn't, to you. It smacks of weakness to mention such things to the enemy."

"I'm not the enemy."

King smiled. "Aren't you?"

He left his son sitting at the table, deep in thought.

Maddie was working in the yard when the developer drove up a week later. She leaned on the pitchfork she was using to put hay into a trough, and waited, miserable, for him to get out of his car and talk to her.

"I won't sell," she said when he came up to her. "And in case you feel like high pressure tactics, my neighbor has mounted cameras all over the ranch." She flushed at his fury.

"Well, how about that?" he drawled, and his eyes were blazing with anger. He forced a smile. "You did know that cameras can be disabled?" he asked.

"The cameras also have listening devices that can pick up a whisper."

He actually seemed to go pale. He looked at the poles that contained the outside lighting and mumbled a curse under his breath. There was some sort of electronic device up there.

"I'll come back again one day and ask you the same question," he promised, but he smiled and his voice was pleasant. "Maybe you'll change your mind."

"We also have cowboys in the line cabins on the borders of this ranch. Mr. Brannt is very protective of me since my father died. He buys many of our young breeding bulls," she added for good measure.

He was very still. "King Brannt?"

"Yes. You've heard of him, I gather."

He didn't reply. He turned on his heel and marched back to his car. But this time he didn't spin his wheels.

Maddie almost fell over with relief.

Just as the developer left, another car drove up, a sleek Jaguar, black with silver trim. Maddie didn't recognize it. Oh, dear, didn't some hit men drive fancy cars . . . ?

The door opened and big John Everett climbed out of the low-slung luxury car, holding on to his white Stetson so that it wouldn't be dislodged from his thick head of blond hair. Maddie almost laughed with relief.

John grinned as he approached her. He had pale blue eyes, almost silver-colored, like his dad's, and he was a real dish. He and Odalie both had their mother's blond fairness, instead of Cole Everett's dark hair and olive complexion.

"What the hell's wrong with you?" he drawled. "Black cars make you twitchy or something?"

"I think hit men drive them, is all."

He burst out laughing. "I've never shot one

single person. A deer or two, maybe, in season." He moved toward her and stopped, towering over her. His pale eyes were dancing on her flushed face. "I ran into King Brannt at a cattlemen's association meeting last night. He said you were having some problems trying to work out your father's breeding program. He said Cort explained it to you."

"Uh, well, yes, sort of." It was hard to admit that even taking notes, she hadn't understood much of what Cort had told her.

"Cort tried to tutor me in biology in high school. I got a D on the test. He's good at genetics, lousy at trying to explain them." He shoved his hat back on his head and grinned. "So I thought, maybe I'll come over and have a try at helping you understand it."

"You're a nice guy, John," she said gently. And he was. At the height of his sister's intimidation, John had been on Maddie's side.

He shrugged. "I'm the flower of my family." His face hardened. "Even if she is my sister, Odalie makes me ashamed sometimes. I haven't forgotten the things she did to you."

"We all make mistakes when we're young," she faltered, trying to be fair.

"You have a gentle nature," he observed. "Like Cort's mother. And mine," he added with a smile. "Mom can't bear to see anything hurt. She cried for days when your father's lawyer came over and told her and Dad what Odalie had done to you."

"I know. She called me. Your dad did, too. They're good people."

"Odalie might be a better person if she had a few disadvantages," John said coldly. "As things stand, she'll give in to Cort's persuasion one day and marry him. He'll be in hell for the rest of his life. The only person she's ever really loved is herself."

"That's harsh, John," she chided gently.

"It's the truth, Maddie." He swung his pointing finger at her nose. "You're like my mother . . . she'd find one nice thing to say about the devil." He smiled. "I'm in the mood to do some tutoring today. But I require payment. Your great-aunt makes a mean cup of coffee, and I'm partial to French vanilla."

"That's my favorite."

He chuckled. "Mine, too." He went back to the car, opened the passenger seat, took out a big box and a bag. "So since I drink a lot of it, I brought my own."

She caught her breath. It was one of those European coffee machines that used pods. Maddie had always wanted one, but the price was prohibitive.

"Sad thing is it only brews one cup at a time, but we'll compensate." He grinned. "So lead the way to the kitchen and I'll show you how to use it."

71

· · ·

Two cups of mouthwatering coffee later, they were sitting in Maddie's father's office, going over breeding charts. John found the blackboard her father had used to map out the genetics. He was able to explain it so simply that Maddie understood almost at once which herd sires to breed to which cows.

"You make it sound so simple!" she exclaimed. "You're a wonder, John!"

He laughed. "It's all a matter of simplification," he drawled. He leaned back in the chair and sketched Maddie's radiant face with narrowed pale blue eyes. "You sell yourself short. It's not that you can't understand. You just have to have things explained. Cort's too impatient."

She averted her eyes. Mention of Cort made her uneasy.

"Yes, he loses his temper," John said thoughtfully. "But he's not dangerous. Not like that boy."

She paled. "I can't talk about it."

"You can, and you should," he replied solemnly. "Your father was advised to get some counseling for you, but he didn't believe in such things. That boy had a record for domestic assault, did you ever know? He beat his grandmother almost to death one day. She refused to press charges, or he would have gone to jail. His parents jumped in and got a fancy lawyer and convinced the authorities that he wasn't dangerous. I believe they contributed to the reelection campaign of the man who was police chief at the time as well."

"That's a harsh accusation," she said, shocked.

"It's a harsh world, and politics is the dirtiest business in town. Corruption doesn't stop at criminals, you know. Rich people have a way of subverting justice from time to time."

"You're rich, and you don't do those types of things."

"Yes, I am rich," he replied honestly. "And I'm honest. I have my own business, but I didn't get where I am by depending on my dad to support me."

She searched his eyes curiously. "Is that a dig at Cort?"

"It is," he replied quietly. "He stays at home, works on the ranch and does what King tells him to do. I told him some time ago that he's hurting himself by doing no more than wait to inherit Skylance, but he just nods and walks off."

"Somebody will have to take over the ranch when King is too old to manage it," she pointed out reasonably. "There isn't anybody else."

John grimaced. "I suppose that's true. But it's the same with me. Can you really see Odalie running a ranch?" He burst out laughing. "God, she might chip a fingernail!"

She grinned from ear to ear.

"Anyway, I was a maverick. I wanted my own

business. I have a farm-equipment business and I also specialize in marketing native grasses for pasture improvement."

"You're an entrepreneur," she said with a chuckle.

"Something like that, I guess." He cocked his head and studied her. "You know I don't date much."

"Yes. Sort of like me. I'm not modern enough for most men."

"I'm not modern enough for most women," he replied, and smiled. "Uh, there's going to be a dressy party over at the Hancock place to introduce a new rancher in the area. I wondered if you might like to go with me?"

"A party?" she asked. She did have one good dress. She'd bought it for a special occasion a while ago, and she couldn't really afford another one with the ranch having financial issues. But it was a nice dress. Her eyes brightened. "I haven't been to a party in a long time. I went with Dad to a conference in Denver before he got sick."

"I remember. You looked very nice."

"Well, I'd be wearing the same dress I had on then," she pointed out.

He laughed. "I don't follow the current fashions for women," he mused. "I'm inviting you, not the dress."

"In that case," she said with a pert smile, "I'd be delighted!"

Chapter Four

Some men dragged their feet around the room and called it dancing. John Everett could actually dance! He knew all the Latin dances and how to waltz, although he was uncomfortable with some of the newer ways to display on a dance floor. Fortunately the organizers of the party were older people and they liked older music.

Only a minute into an enthusiastic samba, John and Maddie found themselves in the middle of the dance floor with the other guests clapping as they marked the fast rhythm.

"We should take this show on the road." John chuckled as they danced.

"I'm game. I'll give up ranching and become a professional samba performer, if you'll come, too," she suggested.

"Maybe only part of the year," he mused. "We can't let our businesses go to pot."

"Spoilsport."

He grinned.

While the two were dancing, oblivious to the other guests, a tall, dark man in a suit walked in and found himself a flute of champagne. He tasted it, nodding to other guests. Everyone was gathered around the dance floor of the ballroom in the Victorian mansion. He wandered to the fringes and caught his breath. There, on the dance floor, was Maddie Lane.

She was wearing a dress, a sheath of black slinky material that dipped in front to display just a hint of the lovely curve of her breasts and display her long elegant neck and rounded arms. Her pale blond hair shone like gold in the light from the chandeliers. She was wearing makeup, just enough to enhance what seemed to be a rather pretty face, and the pretty calves of her legs were displayed to their best advantage from the arch of her spiked high-heel shoes. He'd rarely seen her dressed up. Not that he'd been interested in her or anything.

But there she was, decked out like a Christmas tree, dancing with his best friend. John didn't date anybody. Until now.

Cort Brannt felt irritation rise in him like bile. He scowled at the display they were making of themselves. Had they no modesty at all? And people were clapping like idiots.

He glared at Maddie. He remembered the last time he'd seen her. She backed away from Cort, but she was dancing with John as if she really liked him. Her face was radiant. She was smiling. Cort had rarely seen her smile at all. Of course, usually he was yelling at her or making hurtful remarks. Not much incentive for smiles.

He sipped champagne. Someone spoke to him. He just nodded. He was intent on the dancing couple, focused and furious.

Suddenly he noticed that the flute was empty. He turned and went back to the hors d'oeuvres table and had them refill it. But he didn't go back to the dance floor. Instead he found a fellow cattleman to talk to about the drought and selling off cattle.

A few minutes later he was aware of two people helping themselves to punch and cake.

"Oh, hi, Cort," John greeted him with a smile. "I didn't think you were coming."

"Hadn't planned to," Cort said in a cool tone. "My dad had an emergency on the ranch, so I'm filling in. One of the officers of the cattlemen's association is here." He indicated the man with a nod of his head. "Dad wanted me to ask him about any pending legislation that might help us through the drought. We've heard rumors, but nothing substantial."

"My dad was wondering the same." John frowned. "You okay?"

"I'm fine," Cort said, making sure that he enunciated as plainly as possible. He stood taller, although he still wasn't as tall, or as big, as his friend. "Why do you ask?"

"Because that's your second glass of champagne and you don't drink," John said flatly.

Cort held the flute up and looked at it. It was

empty. "Where did that go?" he murmured.

"Just a guess, but maybe you drank it?" John replied.

Cort set the flute on the spotless white table-cloth and looked down at Maddie. "You're keeping expensive company these days."

She was shocked at the implication.

"Hold it right there," John said, and his deep tone was menacing. "I invited her."

"Got plans, have you?" Cort replied coldly.

"Why shouldn't I?" came the droll reply. "Oh, by the way, Odalie says her Italian voice teacher is an idiot. He doesn't know beans about how to sing, and he isn't teaching her anything. So she thinks she may come home soon."

Maddie felt her heart sink. Cort's expression lightened. "You think she might?"

"It's possible. You should lay off that stuff."

Cort glanced at the flute. "I suppose so."

"Hey, John, can I talk to you for a minute?" a man called to him. "I need a new combine!"

"I need a new sale," John teased. He glanced at Maddie. "I won't be a minute, okay?"

"Okay," she said. But she was clutching her small evening bag as if she was afraid that it might escape. She started looking around for someone, anyone, to talk to besides Cort Brannt.

While she was thinking about running, he slid his big hand into her small one and pulled her onto the dance floor. He didn't even ask. He folded her into his arms and led her to the lazy, slow rhythm.

He smelled of spicy, rich cologne. He was much taller than she was, so she couldn't see his face. She felt his cheek against the big wave of blond hair at her temple and her body began to do odd things. She felt uneasy, nervous. She felt . . . safe, excited.

"Your hand is like ice," he murmured as he danced with her around the room.

"They get cold all the time," she lied.

He laughed deep in his throat. "Really."

She wondered why he was doing this. Surely he should be pleased about Odalie's imminent reappearance in his life. He hated Maddie. Why was he dancing with her?

"I've never raised my hand to a woman," he said at her ear. "I never would, no matter how angry I was."

She swallowed and stopped dancing. She didn't want to talk about that.

He coaxed her eyes up. His were dark, narrow, intent. He was remembering what his father had told him, about the boy who tried to throw Maddie out a second-story window because of Odalie's lies. He didn't want to believe that Odalie had meant that to happen. Surely her female visitor had talked her into putting those nasty things about the boy and his family on the internet. But however it had happened, the thought of someone manhandling Maddie made him angry. It upset him.

He didn't really understand why. He'd never thought of her in any romantic way. She was just Pierce Lane's daughter. He'd known her since she was a child, watched her follow her dad around the ranch. She was always petting a calf or a dog, or carrying chickens around because she liked the sounds they made.

"Why are you watching me like that?" she faltered.

"You love animals, don't you?" he asked, and there was an odd, soft glow about his dark eyes. "I remember you carrying Mom's chickens around like cuddly toys when you'd come over to the ranch with your dad. You were very small then. I had to rescue you from one of the herding dogs. You tried to pet him, and he wasn't a pet."

"His name was Rowdy," she recalled. "He was so pretty."

"We never let anybody touch those dogs except the man who trains and uses them. They have to be focused. You didn't know." He smiled. "You were a cute little kid. Always asking questions, always curious about everything."

She shifted uncomfortably. He wasn't dancing and they were drawing attention.

He looked around, cocked an eyebrow and moved her back around the room in his arms. "Sorry."

She didn't know what to think. She was tingling all over. She wanted him to hold her so close that she could feel every inch of his powerful frame against her. She wanted him to bend his head and kiss her so hard that her lips would sting. She wanted . . . something. Something more. She didn't understand these new and unexpected longings. It was getting hard to breathe and her heartbeat was almost shaking her. She couldn't bear it if he noticed.

He did notice. She was like melting ice in his arms. He felt her shiver when he drew her even closer, so that her soft, pert little breasts were hard against his chest through the thin suit jacket he was wearing. He liked the way she smelled, of wildflowers in the sun.

He drank in that scent. It made his head swim. His arm contracted. He was feeling sensations that he'd almost forgotten. Odalie didn't like him close to her, so his longing for her had been stifled. But Maddie was soft and warm and receptive. Too receptive.

His mouth touched her ear. "You make me hungry," he whispered roughly.

"Ex-excuse me?" she stammered.

"I want to lay you down on the carpet and kiss your breasts until my body stops hurting."

She caught her breath and stopped dancing. She pushed back from him, her eyes blazing, her face red with embarrassment. She wanted to kick him in the shin, but that would cause more problems.

She turned away from him, almost shivering with the emotions he'd kindled in her, shocked at the things he'd said to her. She almost ran toward John, who was walking toward her, frowning.

"What is it?" he asked suddenly, putting his arm around her.

She hid her face against him.

He glared at Cort, who was approaching them with more conflicting emotions than he'd ever felt in his life.

"You need to go home," John told Cort in a patient tone that was belied by his expression. "You've had too much to drink and you're going to make a spectacle of yourself and us if you keep this up."

"I want to dance with her," Cort muttered stubbornly.

"Well, it's pretty obvious that she doesn't want to dance with you." John leaned closer. "I can pick you up over my shoulder and carry you out of here, and I will."

"I'd like to see you try it," Cort replied, and his eyes blazed with anger.

Another cattleman, seeing a confrontation building, came strolling over and deliberately got between the two men.

"Hey, Cort," he said pleasantly, "I need to ask you about those new calves your dad's going to put up at the fall production sale. Can I ride home with you and see them?"

Cort blinked. "It's the middle of the night."

"The barn doesn't have lights?" the older man asked, raising an eyebrow.

Cort was torn. He knew the man. He was from up around the Frio river. He had a huge ranch, and Cort's dad was hungry for new customers.

"The barn has lights. I guess we could . . . go look at the calves." He was feeling very light-headed. He wasn't used to alcohol. Not at all.

"I'll drive you home," the rancher said gently. "You can have one of your cowboys fetch your car, can't you?"

"Yeah. I guess so."

"Thanks," John told the man.

He shrugged and smiled. "No problem."

He indicated the door. Cort hesitated for just a minute. He looked back at Maddie with dark, stormy eyes, long enough that she dropped her own like hot bricks. He gave John a smug glance and followed the visiting cattleman out the door.

"Oh, boy," John said to himself. "Now we get to the complications."

"Complications?" Maddie was only half listening. Her eyes were on Cort's long, elegant back. She couldn't remember ever being so confused.

After the party was over, John drove her to her front door and cut off the engine.

"What happened?" he asked her gently, because she was still visibly upset.

"Cort was out of line," she murmured without lifting her eyes.

"Not surprising. He doesn't drink. I can't imagine what got him started."

"I guess he's missing your sister," she replied with a sigh. She looked up at him. "She's really coming home?"

"She says she is," he told her. He made a face. "That's Odalie. She always knows more than anybody else about any subject. My parents let her get away with being sassy because she was pretty and talented." He laughed shortly. "My dad let me have it if I was ever rude or impolite or spoke out of turn. My brother had it even rougher."

She cocked her head. "You never talk about Tanner."

He grimaced. "I can't. It's a family thing. Maybe I'll tell you one day. Anyway, Dad pulled me up short if I didn't toe the line at home." He shook his head. "You wouldn't believe how many times I had to clean the horse stalls when I made him mad."

"Odalie is beautiful," Maddie conceded, but in a subdued tone.

"Only a very few people know what she did to you," John said quietly. "It shamed the family. Odalie was only sorry she got caught. I think she finally realized how tragic the results could have been, though."

"How so?"

"For one thing, she never spoke again to the girlfriend who put her up to it," he said. "After she got out of school, she stopped posting on her social page and threw herself into studying music."

"The girlfriend moved away, didn't she, though?"

"She moved because threats were made. Legal ones," John confided. "My dad sent his attorneys after her. He was pretty sure that Odalie didn't know how to link internet sites and post simultaneously, which is what was done about you." He touched her short hair gently. "Odalie is spoiled and snobbish and she thinks she's the center of the universe. But she isn't cruel."

"Isn't she?"

"Well, not anymore," he added. "Not since the lawyers got involved. You weren't the only girl she victimized. Several others came forward and talked to my dad when they heard about what happened to you in the library. He was absolutely dumbfounded. So was my mother." He shook his head. "Odalie never got over what they said to her. She started making a real effort to consider the feelings of other people. Years too late, of course, and she's still got that bad attitude."

"It's a shame she isn't more like your mother," Maddie said gently, and she smiled. "Mrs. Everett is a sweet woman."

"Yes. Mom has an amazing voice and is not conceited. She was offered a career in opera but she turned it down. She liked singing the blues, she said. Now, she just plays and sings for us, and composes. There's still the occasional journalist who shows up at the door when one of her songs is a big hit, like Desperado's."

"Do they still perform . . . I mean Desperado?" she qualified.

"Yes, but not so much. They've all got kids now. It makes it tough to go on the road, except during summer holidays."

She laughed. "I love their music."

"Me, too." He studied her. "Odd."

"What is?"

"You're so easy to talk to. I don't get along with most women. I'm strung up and nervous and the aggressive ones make me uncomfortable. I sort of gave up dating after my last bad experience." He laughed. "I don't like women making crude remarks to me."

"Isn't it funny how things have changed?" she wondered aloud. "Not that I'm making fun of you. It's just that women used to get hassled. They still do, but it's turned around somewhat—now men get it, too."

"Yes, life is much more complicated now."

"I really enjoyed the party. Especially the dancing."

"Me, too. We might do that again one day."

She raised both eyebrows. "We might?"

He chuckled. "I'll call you."

"That would be nice."

He smiled, got out, went around and opened the door for her. He seemed to be debating whether or not to kiss her. She liked that lack of aggression in him. She smiled, went on tiptoe and kissed him right beside his chiseled mouth.

"Thanks again," she said. "See you!"

She went up the steps and into the house. John Everett stood looking after her wistfully. She thought he was nice. She liked him. But when she'd come off the dance floor trailing Cort Brannt, she'd been radiating like a furnace. Whether she knew it or not, she was in love with Cort. Shame, he thought as he drove off. She was just the sort of woman he'd like to settle down with. Not much chance of that, now.

Maddie didn't sleep at all. She stared at the ceiling. Her body tingled from the long contact with Cort's. She could feel his breath on her forehead, his lips in her hair. She could hear what he'd whispered.

She flushed at the memory. It had evoked incredible hunger. She didn't understand why she had these feelings now, when she hadn't had them for that boy who'd tried to hurt her so badly. She'd really thought she was crazy about him. But it was nothing like this.

Since her bad experience, she hadn't dated

much. She'd seen her father get mad, but it was always quick and never physical. She hadn't been exposed to men who hit women. Now she knew they existed. It had been a worrying discovery.

Cort had frightened her when he'd lost his temper so violently in her father's office. She didn't think he'd attack her. But she'd been wary of him, until they danced together. Even if he was drunk, it had been the experience of a lifetime. She thought she could live on it forever, even if Odalie came home and Cort married her. He was never going to be happy with her, though. Odalie loved herself so much that there was no room in her life for a man.

If only the other woman had fallen in love with the Italian voice trainer and married him. Then Cort would have to let go of his unrequited feelings for Odalie, and maybe look in another direction. Maybe look in Maddie's direction.

On the other hand, he'd only been teasing at the dance. He wasn't himself.

Cold sober, he'd never have anything to do with Maddie. Probably, he'd just been missing Odalie and wanted a warm body to hold. Yes. That was probably it.

Just before dawn she fell asleep, but all too soon it was time to get up and start doing the chores around the ranch.

She went to feed her flock of hens, clutching the

metal garbage can lid and the leafy limb to fend off Pumpkin. Somewhere in the back of her mind, she realized that it was going to come down to a hard decision one day. Pumpkin protected her hens, yes; he would be the bane of predators everywhere. But he was equally dangerous to people. What if he flew up and got one of her cowboys in the eye? She'd been reading up on rooster behavior, and she'd read some horror stories.

There had been all sorts of helpful advice, like giving him special treats and being nice to him. That had resulted in more gouges on her legs, even through her slacks, where his spurs had landed. Then there was the advice about having his spurs trimmed. Good advice, but who was going to catch and hold him while someone did that? None of her cowboys were lining up to volunteer.

"You problem child," she told Pumpkin as he chased her toward the gate. "One day, I'll have to do something about you!"

She got through the gate in the nick of time and shut it, hard. At least he wasn't going to get out of there, she told herself. She'd had Ben go around the perimeter of the large fenced area that surrounded the henhouse and plug any openings where that sneaky feathered fiend could possibly get out. If she kept him shut up, he couldn't hurt anybody, and the fence was seven feet high. No way he was jumping that!

She said so to Ben as she made her way to the barn to check on a calf they were nursing; it had dropped late and its mother had been killed by predators. They found it far on the outskirts of the ranch. They couldn't figure how it had wandered so far, but then, cattle did that. It was why you brought pregnant cows up close to the barn, so that you'd know when they were calving. It was especially important to do that in winter, just before the spring calves were due.

She looked over the gate at the little calf in the stall and smiled. "Pretty boy," she teased.

He was a purebred Santa Gertrudis bull. Some were culled and castrated and became steers, if they had poor conformation or were less than robust. But the best ones were treated like cattle royalty, spoiled rotten and watched over. This little guy would one day bring a handsome price as a breeding bull.

She heard a car door slam and turned just as Cort came into the barn.

She felt her heartbeat shoot off like a rocket.

He tilted his hat back and moved to the stall, peering over it. "That's a nice young one," he remarked.

"His mother was killed, so we're nursing him," she faltered.

He frowned. "Killed?"

"Predators, we think," she replied. "She was pretty torn up. We found her almost at the highway, out near your line cabin. Odd, that she wandered so far."

"Very odd," he agreed.

Ben came walking in with a bottle. " 'Day, Cort," he said pleasantly.

"How's it going, Ben?" the younger man replied.

"So far so good."

Maddie smiled as Ben settled down in the hay and fed the bottle to the hungry calf.

"Poor little guy," Maddie said.

"He'll make it," Ben promised, smiling up at her.

"Well, I'll leave you to it," Maddie said. She was reluctant to be alone with Cort after the night before, but she couldn't see any way around it.

"You're up early," she said, fishing for a safe topic.

"I didn't sleep." He stuck his hands into his pockets as he strolled along with her toward the house.

"Oh?"

He stopped, so that she had to. His eyes were bloodshot and they had dark circles under them. "I drank too much," he said. "I wanted to apologize for the way I behaved with you."

"Oh." She looked around for anything more than one syllable that she could reply with. "That's . . . that's okay."

He stared down at her with curiously intent eyes. "You're incredibly naive."

She averted her eyes and her jaw clenched. "Yes, well, with my background, you'd probably be the same way. I haven't been anxious to repeat the mistakes of the past with some other man who wasn't what he seemed to be."

"I'm sorry. About what happened to you."

"Everybody was sorry," she replied heavily. "But nobody else has to live with the emotional baggage I'm carrying around."

"How did you end up at the party with John?"

She blinked. "Well, he came over to show me some things about animal husbandry, and he asked me to go with him. It was sort of surprising, really. He doesn't date anybody."

"He's had a few bad experiences with women. So have I."

She'd heard about Cort's, but she wasn't opening that topic with him. "Would you like coffee?" she asked. "Great-Aunt Sadie went shopping, but she left a nice coffee cake baking in the oven. It should be about ready."

"Thanks. I could use a second cup," he added with a smile.

But the smile faded when he saw the fancy European coffee machine on the counter. "Where the hell did you buy that?" he asked.

She flushed. "I didn't. John likes European

coffee, so he brought the machine and the pods over with him."

He lifted his chin. "Did he, now? I gather he thinks he'll be having coffee here often, then?"

She frowned. "He didn't say anything about that."

He made a huffing sound in his throat, just as the stove timer rang. Maddie went to take the coffee cake out of the oven. She was feeling so rattled, it was a good thing she'd remembered that it was baking. She placed it on a trivet. It smelled of cinnamon and butter.

"My great-aunt can really cook," she remarked as she took off the oven mitts she'd used to lift it out.

"She can, can't she?"

She turned and walked right into Cort. She hadn't realized he was so close. He caught her small waist in his big hands and lifted her right onto the counter next to the coffee cake, so that she was even with his dark, probing eyes.

"You looked lovely last night," he said in a strange, deep tone. "I've never really seen you dressed up before."

"I . . . I don't dress up," she stammered. He was tracing her collarbone and the sensations it aroused were delicious and unsettling. "Just occasionally."

"I didn't know you could do those complicated Latin dances, either," he continued.

"I learned them from watching television," she said.

His head was lower now. She could feel his breath on her lips; feel the heat from his body as he moved closer, in between her legs so that he was right up against her.

"I'm not in John Everett's class as a dancer," he drawled, tilting her chin up. "But, then, he's not in my class . . . at this . . ."

His mouth slowly covered hers, teasing gently, so that he didn't startle her. He tilted her head just a little more, so that her mouth was at just the right angle. His firm lips pushed hers apart, easing them back, so that he had access to the soft, warm depths of her mouth.

He kissed her with muted hunger, so slowly that she didn't realize until too late how much a trap it was. He grew insistent then, one lean hand at the back of her head, holding it still, as his mouth devoured her soft lips.

"Sweet," he whispered huskily. "You taste like honey. . . ."

His arms went under hers and around her, lifting her, so that her breasts were flattened against his broad, strong chest.

Involuntarily her cold hands snaked around his neck. She'd never felt hunger like this. She hadn't known it was possible. She let him open her mouth with his, let him grind her breasts against him. She moaned softly as sensations she'd never experienced left her helpless, vulnerable.

She felt his hand in her hair, tangling in it, while he kissed her in the soft silence of the kitchen. It was a moment out of time when she wished it could never end, that she could go on kissing him forever.

But just when he lifted his head, and looked into her eyes, and started to speak . . .

A car pulled up at the front porch and a door slammed.

Maddie looked into Cort's eyes with shock. He seemed almost as unsettled as she did. He moved back, helping her off the counter and onto her feet. He backed up just as Great-Aunt Sadie walked in with two bags of groceries.

"Didn't even have fresh mushrooms, can you believe it?" she was moaning, her mind on the door that was trying to close in her face rather than the two dazed people in the kitchen.

"Here, let me have those," Cort said politely, and he took the bags and put them on the counter. "Are there more in the car?" he asked.

"No, but thank you, Cort," Sadie said with a warm smile.

He grinned. "No problem." He glanced at Maddie, who still looked rattled. "I have to go. Thanks for the offer of coffee. Rain check?" he added, and his eyes were almost black with feeling.

"Oh, yes," Maddie managed breathlessly. "Rain check."

He smiled at her and left her standing there, vibrating with new hope.

Chapter Five

Maddie still couldn't believe what had happened right there in her kitchen. Cort had kissed her, and as if he really did feel something for her. Besides that, he was very obviously jealous of John Everett. She felt as if she could actually walk on air.

"You look happier than I've seen you in years, sweetie," Great-Aunt Sadie said with a smile.

"I am."

Sadie grinned. "It's that John Everett, isn't it?" she teased. She indicated the coffeemaker. "Thought he was pretty interested. I mean, those things cost the earth. Not every man would start out courting a girl with a present like that!"

"Oh. Well, of course, I like John," Maddie stammered. And then she realized that she couldn't very well tell her great-aunt what was going on. Sadie might start gossiping. Maddie's ranch hands had friends who worked for the Brannts. She didn't want Cort to think she was telling tales about him, even in an innocent way. After all, it might have been a fluke. He could be missing Odalie and just reacted to Maddie in unexpected ways.

"He's a dish," Sadie continued as she peeled potatoes in the kitchen. "Handsome young man, just like his dad." She grimaced. "I'm not too fond of his sister, but, then, no family is perfect."

"No." She hesitated. "Sadie, do you know why nobody talks about the oldest brother, Tanner?"

Sadie smiled. "Just gossip. They said he and his dad had a major falling out over his choice of careers and he packed up and went to Europe. That was when he was in his late teens. As far as I know, he's never contacted the family since. It's a sore spot with the Everetts, so they don't talk about him anymore. Too painful, I expect."

"That's sad."

"Yes, it is. There was a rumor that he was hanging out with some dangerous people as well. But you know what rumors are."

"Yes," Maddie said.

"What was Cort doing over here earlier in the week?" Sadie asked suddenly.

"Oh, he was just . . . giving me some more pointers on dad's breeding program," Maddie lied.

"Scared you to death, too," Sadie said irritably. "I don't think he'd hurt you, but he's got a bad temper, sweetie."

Maddie had forgotten that, in the new relationship she seemed to be building with Cort. "People say his father was like that, when he was young. But Shelby married him and tamed him," she added with a secret smile.

Sadie glanced at her curiously. "I guess that can happen. A good woman can be the salvation of a man. But just . . . be careful."

"I will," she promised. "Cort isn't a mean person."

Sadie gave her a careful look. "So that's how it is."

Maddie flushed. "I don't know what you mean."

"John likes you, a lot," she replied.

Maddie sighed. "John's got a barracuda for a sister, too," she reminded the older woman. "No way in the world am I having her for a sister-in-law, no matter how nice John is."

Sadie grimaced. "Should have thought of that, shouldn't I?"

"I did."

She laughed. "I guess so. But just a suggestion, if you stick your neck out with Cort," she added very seriously. "Make him mad. Make him really mad, someplace where you can get help if you need to. Don't wait and find out when it's too late if he can't control his temper."

"I remember that boy in high school," Maddie reminded her. "He didn't stop. Cort frightened me, yes, but when he saw I was afraid, he started apologizing. If he couldn't control his temper, he'd never have been able to stop."

Sadie looked calmer. "No. I don't think he would."

"He's still apologizing for it, in fact," Maddie added.

Sadie smiled and her eyes were kind. "All right, then. I won't harp on it. He's a lot like his father, and his dad is a good man."

"They're all nice people. Morie was wonderful to me in school. She stuck up for me when Odalie and her girlfriend were making my life a daily purgatory."

"Pity Odalie never really gets paid back for the things she does," Sadie muttered.

Maddie hugged her. "That mill grinds slowly but relentlessly," she reminded her. She grinned. "One day . . ."

Sadie laughed. "One day."

Maddie let her go with a sigh. "I hope I can learn enough of this stuff not to sink dad's cattle operation," she moaned. "I wasn't really faced with having to deal with the breeding aspect until now, with roundup ahead and fall breeding standing on the line in front of me. Which bull do I put on which cows? Gosh! It's enough to drive you nuts!"

"Getting a lot of help in that, though, aren't you?" Sadie teased. "Did you tell Cort that John had been coaching you, too?"

"Yes." She sighed. "Cort wasn't overjoyed about it, either. But John makes it understandable." She threw up her hands. "I'm just slow. I don't understand cattle. I love to paint and sculpt. But Dad never expected to go so soon and have to leave me in charge of things. We're going in the hole because I don't know what I'm doing." She glanced at the older woman. "In about two years, we're going to start losing customers. It terrifies me. I don't want to lose the ranch, but it's going to go downhill without dad to run it." She toyed with a bag on the counter. "I've been thinking about that developer . . ."

"Don't you dare," Sadie said firmly. "Darlin', do you realize what he'd do to this place if he got his hands on it?" she exclaimed. "He'd sell off all the livestock to anybody who wanted it, even for slaughter, and he'd rip the land to pieces. All that prime farmland, gone, all the native grasses your dad planted and nurtured, gone. This house—" she indicated it "—where your father and your grandfather and I were born! Gone!"

Maddie felt sick. "Oh, dear."

"You're not going to run the ranch into the ground. Not when you have people, like King Brannt, who want to help you get it going again," she said firmly. "If you ever want to sell up, you talk to him. I'll bet he'd offer for it and put in a manager. We could probably even stay on and pay rent."

"With what?" Maddie asked reasonably. "Your social security check and my egg money?" She sighed. "I can't sell enough paintings or enough eggs to pay for lunch in town," she added miserably. "I should have gone to school and learned a trade or something." She grimaced. "I don't know what to do."

"Give it a little time," the older woman said gently. "I know it's overwhelming, but you can learn. Ask John to make you a chart and have Ben in on the conversation. Your dad trusted Ben with everything, even the finances. I daresay he knows as much as you do about things."

"That's an idea." She smiled sadly. "I don't really want to sell that developer anything. He's got a shady look about him."

"You're telling me."

"I guess I'll wait a bit."

"Meanwhile, you might look in that bag I brought home yesterday."

"Isn't it groceries . . . dry goods?"

"Look."

She peered in the big brown bag and caught her breath. "Sculpting material. Paint! Great-Aunt Sadie!" she exclaimed, and ran and hugged the other woman. "That's so sweet of you!"

"Looking out for you, darling," she teased. "I want you to be famous so those big TV people will want to interview me on account of we're related!" She stood up and struck a pose. "Don't you think I'd be a hit?"

Maddie hugged her even tighter. "I think you're already a hit. Okay. I can take a hint. I'll get to work right now!"

Sadie chortled as she rushed from the room.

Cort came in several days later while she was retouching one of the four new fairies she'd created, working where the light was best, in a corner of her father's old office. She looked up, startled, when Great-Aunt Sadie let him in.

She froze. "Pumpkin came after you again?" she asked, worried.

"What?" He looked around, as if expecting the big red rooster to appear. "Oh, Pumpkin." He chuckled. "No. He was in the hen yard giving me mean looks, but he seems to be well contained."

"Thank goodness!"

He moved to the table and looked at her handiwork. "What a group," he mused, smiling. "They're all beautiful."

"Thanks." She wished she didn't sound so breathless, and that she didn't have paint dabbed all over her face from her days' efforts. She probably looked like a painting herself.

"Going to sell them?"

"Oh, I couldn't," she said hesitantly. "I mean, I . . . well, I just couldn't."

"Can't you imagine what joy they'd bring to

other people?" he asked, thinking out loud. "Why do you think doll collectors pay so much for one-of-a-kind creations like those? They build special cabinets for them, take them out and talk to them . . ."

"You're kidding!" she exclaimed, laughing. "Really?"

"This one guy I met at the conference said he had about ten really rare dolls. He sat them around the dining room table every night and talked to them while he ate. He was very rich and very eccentric, but you get the idea. He loved his dolls. He goes to all the doll collector conventions. In fact, there's one coming up in Denver, where they're holding a cattlemen's workshop." He smiled. "Anyway, your fairies wouldn't be sitting on a shelf collecting dust on the shelf of a collector like that. They'd be loved."

"Wow." She looked back at the little statuettes. "I never thought of it like that."

"Maybe you should."

She managed a shy smile. He looked delicious in a pair of beige slacks and a yellow, very expensive pullover shirt with an emblem on the pocket. Thick black hair peeked out where the top buttons were undone. She wondered how his bare chest would feel against her hands. She blushed. "What can I do for you?" she asked quickly, trying to hide her interest.

Her reaction to him was amusing. He found it

really touching. Flattering. He hadn't been able to get her out of his mind since he'd kissed her so hungrily in her kitchen. He'd wanted to come back sooner than this, but business had overwhelmed him.

"I have to drive down to Jacobsville, Texas, to see a rancher about some livestock," he said. "I thought you might like to ride with me."

She stared at him as if she'd won the lottery. "Me?"

"You." He smiled. "I'll buy you lunch on the way. I know this little tearoom off the beaten path. We can have high tea and buttermilk pie."

She caught her breath. "I used to hear my mother talk about that one. I've never had high tea. I'm not even sure what it is, exactly."

"Come with me and find out."

She grinned. "Okay! Just let me wash up first."

"Take your time. I'm not in any hurry."

"I'll just be a few minutes."

She almost ran up the staircase to her room.

Cort picked up one of the delicate little fairies and stared at it with utter fascination. It was ethereal, beautiful, stunning. He'd seen such things before, but never anything so small with such personality. The little fairy had short blond hair, like Maddie's, and pale eyes. It amused him that she could paint something so tiny. He noted the magnifying glass standing on the table, and realized that she must use it for the more detailed work. Still, it was like magic, making something so small look so realistic.

He put it down, very carefully, and went into the kitchen to talk to Sadie while he waited for Maddie to get ready.

"Those little fairies she makes are amazing," he commented, lounging against the counter.

Sadie smiled at him. "They really are. I don't know how she does all that tiny detailed work without going blind. The little faces are so realistic. She has a gift."

"She does. I wish she'd do something with it."

"Me, too," Sadie replied. "But she doesn't want to sell her babies, as she calls them."

"She's sitting on a gold mine here." Cort sighed. "You know, breeding herd sires is hard work, even for people who've done it for generations and love it."

She glanced at him and she looked worried. "I know. She doesn't really want to do it. My nephew had to toss her in at the deep end when he knew his cancer was fatal." She shook her head. "I hate it for her. You shouldn't be locked into a job you don't want to do. But she's had no training. She really can't do anything else."

"She can paint. And she can sculpt."

"Yes, but there's still the ranch," Sadie emphasized.

"Any problem has a solution. It's just a

question of finding it." He sighed. "Ben said you'd had another cow go missing."

"Yes." She frowned. "Odd thing, too, she was in a pasture with several other cows, all of them healthier than her. I can't think somebody would steal her."

"I know what you mean. They do wander off. It's just that it looks suspicious, having two go missing in the same month."

"Could it be that developer man?"

Cort shook his head. "I wouldn't think so. We've got armed patrols and cameras mounted everywhere. If anything like that was going on, we'd see it."

"I suppose so."

There was the clatter of footsteps almost leaping down the staircase.

"Okay, I'm ready," Maddie said, breathless. She was wearing jeans and boots and a pretty pink button-up blouse. She looked radiant.

"Where are you off to?" Sadie asked, laughing.

"I'm going to Jacobsville with Cort to look at livestock."

"Oh." Sadie forced a smile. "Well, have fun, then."

Cort started the sleek two-seater Jaguar. He glanced at Maddie, who was looking at everything with utter fascination.

"Not quite like your little Volkswagen, huh?" he teased.

"No! It's like a spaceship or something."

"Watch this."

As he started the car, the air vents suddenly opened up and the Jaguar symbol lit up on a touch screen between the steering wheel and the glove compartment. At the same time, the gearshift rose up from the console, where it had been lying flat.

"Oh, gosh!" she exclaimed. "That's amazing!"

He chuckled. "I like high-tech gadgets."

"John has one of these," she recalled.

His eyes narrowed. "So he does. I rode him around in mine and he found a dealership the next day. His is more sedate."

"I just think they're incredible."

He smiled. "Fasten your seat belt."

"Oops, sorry, wasn't thinking." She reached up and drew it between her breasts, to fasten it beside her hip.

"I always wear my seat belt," he said. "Dad refused to drive the car until we were all strapped in. He was in a wreck once. He said he never forgot that he'd be dead except for the seat belt."

"My dad wasn't in a wreck, but he was always careful about them, too." She put her strappy purse on the floorboard. "Did Odalie come home?" she asked, trying not to sound too interested.

"Not yet," he said. He had to hide a smile, because the question lacked any subtlety.

"Oh."

He was beginning to realize that Odalie had

been a major infatuation for him. Someone unreachable that he'd dreamed about, much as young boys dreamed about movie stars. He knew somewhere in the back of his mind that he and Odalie were as different as night and day. She wanted an operatic career and wasn't interested in fitting him into that picture. Would he be forever hanging around opera houses where she performed, carrying bags and organizing fans? Or would he be in Texas, waiting for her rare visits? She couldn't have a family and be a performer, not in the early stages of her career, maybe never. Cort wanted a family. He wanted children.

Funny, he'd never thought of himself as a parent before. But when he'd listened to Maddie talk about her little fairy sculptures and spoke of them as her children, he'd pictured her with a baby in her arms. It had shocked him how much he wanted to see that for real.

"You like kids, don't you?" he asked suddenly.

"What brought that on?" She laughed.

"What you said, about your little fairy sculptures. They're beautiful kids."

"Thanks." She looked out the window at the dry, parched grasslands they were passing through. "Yes, I love kids. Oh, Cort, look at the poor corn crops! That's old Mr. Raines's land, isn't it?" she added. "He's already holding on to his place by his fingernails. I guess he'll have to sell if it doesn't rain."

"My sister said they're having the same issues up in Wyoming." He glanced at her. "Her husband knows a medicine man from one of the plains tribes. She said that he actually did make it rain a few times. Nobody understands how, and most people think it's fake, but I wonder."

"Ben was talking about a Cheyenne medicine man who can make rain. He's friends with him. I've known people who could douse for water," she said.

"Now, there's a rare talent indeed," he commented. He pursed his lips. "Can't Ben do that?"

"Shh," she said, laughing. "He doesn't want people to think he's odd, so he doesn't want us to tell anybody."

"Still, you might ask him to go see if he could find water. If he does, we could send a well-borer over to do the job for him."

She looked at him with new eyes. "That's really nice of you."

He shrugged. "I'm nice enough. From time to time." He glanced at her pointedly. "When women aren't driving me to drink."

"What? I didn't drive you to drink!"

"The hell you didn't," he mused, his eyes on the road so that he missed her blush. "Dancing with John Everett. Fancy dancing. Latin dancing." He sighed. "I can't even do a waltz."

"Oh, but that doesn't matter," she faltered, trying to deal with the fact that he was jealous.

Was he? That was how it sounded! "I mean, I think you dance very nicely."

"I said some crude things to you," he said heavily. "I'm really sorry. I don't drink, you see. When I do . . ." He let the sentence trail off. "Anyway, I apologize."

"You already apologized."

"Yes, but it weighs on my conscience." He stopped at a traffic light. He glanced at her with dark, soft eyes. "John's my friend. I think a lot of him. But I don't like him taking you out on dates and hanging around you."

She went beet-red. She didn't even know what to say.

"I thought it might come as a shock," he said softly. He reached a big hand across the console and caught hers in it. He linked her fingers with his and looked into her eyes while he waited for the lights to change. "I thought we might take in a movie Friday night. There's that new Batman one."

"There's that new Ice Age one," she said at the same time.

He gave her a long, amused look. "You like cartoon movies?"

She flushed. "Well . . ."

He burst out laughing. "So do I. Dad thinks I'm nuts."

"Oh, I don't!"

His fingers contracted around hers. "Well, in that case, we'll see the Ice Age one."

"Great!"

The light changed and he drove on. But he didn't let go of her hand.

High tea was amazing! There were several kinds of tea, china cups and saucers to contain it, and little cucumber sandwiches, chicken salad sandwiches, little cakes and other nibbles. Maddie had never seen anything like it. The tearoom was full, too, with tourists almost overflowing out of the building, which also housed an antique shop.

"This is awesome!" she exclaimed as she sampled one thing after another.

"Why, thank you." The owner laughed, pausing by their table. "We hoped it would be a success." She shook her head. "Everybody thought we were crazy. We're from Charleston, South Carolina. We came out here when my husband was stationed in the air force base at San Antonio, and stayed. We'd seen another tearoom, way north, almost in Dallas, and we were so impressed with it that we thought we might try one of our own. Neither of us knew a thing about restaurants, but we learned, with help from our staff." She shook her head. "Never dreamed we'd have this kind of success," she added, looking around. "It's quite a dream come true."

"That cameo," Maddie said hesitantly, nodding toward a display case close by. "Does it have a story?"

"A sad one. The lady who owned it said it was

111

handed down in her family for five generations. Finally there was nobody to leave it to. She fell on hard times and asked me to sell it for her." She sighed. "She died a month ago." She opened the case with a key and pulled out the cameo, handing it to Maddie. It was black lacquer with a beautiful black-haired Spanish lady painted on it. She had laughing black eyes and a sweet smile. "She was so beautiful."

"It was the great-great-grandmother of the owner. They said a visiting artist made it and gave it to her. She and her husband owned a huge ranch, from one of those Spanish land grants. Pity there's nobody to keep the legend going."

"Oh, but there is." Cort took it from the woman and handed it to Maddie. "Put it on the tab, if you will," he told the owner. "I can't think of anyone who'll take better care of her."

"No, you can't," Maddie protested, because she saw the price tag.

"I can," Cort said firmly. "It was a family legacy. It still is." His dark eyes stared meaningfully into hers. "It can be handed down, to your own children. You might have a daughter who'd love it one day."

Maddie's heart ran wild. She looked into Cort's dark eyes and couldn't turn away.

"I'll put the ticket with lunch," the owner said with a soft laugh. "I'm glad she'll have a home," she added gently.

"Can you write down the woman's name who sold it to you?" Maddie asked. "I want to remember her, too."

"That I can. How about some buttermilk pie? It's the house specialty," she added with a grin.

"I'd love some."

"Me, too," Cort said.

Maddie touched the beautiful cheek of the cameo's subject. "I should sculpt a fairy who looks like her."

"Yes, you should," Cort agreed at once. "And show it with the cameo."

She nodded. "How sad," she said, "to be the last of your family."

"I can almost guarantee that you won't be the last of yours," he said in a breathlessly tender tone.

She looked up into his face and her whole heart was in her eyes.

He had to fight his first impulse, which was to drag her across the table into his arms and kiss the breath out of her.

She saw that hunger in him and was fascinated that she seemed to have inspired it. He'd said that she was plain and uninteresting. But he was looking at her as if he thought her the most beautiful woman on earth.

"Dangerous," he teased softly, "looking at me like that in a public place."

"Huh?" She caught her breath as she realized

what he was saying. She laughed nervously, put the beautiful cameo beside her plate and smiled at him. "Thank you, for the cameo."

"My pleasure. Eat up. We've still got a long drive ahead of us!"

Jacobsville, Texas, was a place Maddie had heard of all her life, but she'd never seen it before. In the town square, there was a towering statue of Big John Jacobs, the founder of Jacobsville, for whom Jacobs County was named. Legend had it that he came to Texas from Georgia after the Civil War, with a wagonload of black share-croppers. He also had a couple of Comanche men who helped him on the ranch. It was a fascinating story, how he'd married the spunky but not so pretty daughter of a multimillionaire and started a dynasty in Texas.

Maddie shared the history with Cort as they drove down a long dirt road to the ranch, which was owned by Cy Parks. He was an odd sort of person, very reticent, with jet-black hair sprinkled with silver and piercing green eyes. He favored one of his arms, and Maddie could tell that it had been badly burned at some point. His wife was a plain little blonde woman who wore glasses and obviously adored her husband. The feeling seemed to be mutual. They had two sons who were in school, Lisa explained shyly. She was sorry she couldn't introduce them to the visitors.

Cy Parks showed them around his ranch in a

huge SUV. He stopped at one pasture and then another, grimacing at the dry grass.

"We're having to use up our winter hay to feed them," he said with a sigh. "It's going to make it a very hard winter if we have to buy extra feed to carry us through." He glanced at Cort and laughed. "You'll make my situation a bit easier if you want to carry a couple of my young bulls home with you."

Cort grinned, too. "I think I might manage that. Although we're in the same situation you are. Even my sister's husband, who runs purebred cattle in Wyoming, is having it rough. This drought is out of anybody's experience. People are likening it to the famous Dust Bowl of the thirties."

"There was another bad drought in the fifties," Parks added. "When we live on the land, we always have issues with weather, even in good years. This one has been a disaster, though. It will put a lot of the family farms and ranches out of business." He made a face. "They'll be bought up by those damned great combines, corporate ranching, I call it. Animals pumped up with drugs, genetically altered—damned shame. Pardon the language," he added, smiling apologetically at Maddie.

"She's lived around cattlemen all her life," Cort said affectionately, smiling over the back of the seat at her.

"Yes, I have." Maddie laughed. She looked

into Cort's dark eyes and blushed. He grinned.

They stopped at the big barn on the way back and Cy led them through it to a stall in the rear. It connected to a huge paddock with plenty of feed and fresh water.

"Now this is my pride and joy," he said, indicating a sleek, exquisite young Santa Gertrudis bull.

"That is some conformation," Cort said, whistling. "He's out of Red Irony, isn't he?" he added.

Cy chuckled. "So you read the cattle journals, do you?"

"All of them. Your ranch has some of the best breeding stock in Texas. In the country, in fact."

"So does Skylance," Parks replied. "I've bought your own bulls over the years. And your father's," he added to Maddie. "Good stock."

"Thanks," she said.

"Same here," Cort replied. He drew in a breath. "Well, if this little fellow's up for bids, I'll put ours in."

"No bids. He's yours if you want him." He named a price that made Maddie feel faint, but Cort just smiled.

"Done," he said, and they shook hands.

On the way back home, Maddie was still astonished at the price. "That's a fortune," she exclaimed.

"Worth every penny, though," Cort assured her.

"Healthy genetics make healthy progeny. We have to put new bulls on our cows every couple of years to avoid any defects. Too much inbreeding can be dangerous to the cattle and disastrous for us."

"I guess so. Mr. Parks seems like a very nice man," she mused.

He chuckled. "You don't know his history, do you? He led one of the most respected groups of mercenaries in the world into small wars overseas. His friend Eb Scott still runs a world-class counterterrorism school on his ranch. He was part of the merc group, along with a couple of other citizens of Jacobsville."

"I didn't know!"

"He's a good guy. Dad's known him for years."

"What a dangerous way to make a living, though."

"No more dangerous than dealing with livestock," Cort returned.

That was true. There were many pitfalls of working with cattle, the least of which was broken bones. Concussions could be, and sometimes were, fatal. You could drown in a river or be trampled . . . the list went on and on.

"You're very thoughtful," Cort remarked.

She smiled. "I was just thinking."

"Me, too." He turned off onto a side road that led to a park. "I want to stretch my legs for a bit. You game?"

"Of course."

He pulled into the car park and led the way down a small bank to the nearby river. The water level was down, but flowing beautifully over mossy rocks, with mesquite trees drooping a little in the heat, but still pretty enough to catch the eye.

"It's lovely here."

"Yes." He turned and pulled her into his arms, looking down into her wide eyes. "It's very lovely here." He bent his head and kissed her.

Chapter Six

Maddie's head was swimming. She felt the blood rush to her heart as Cort riveted her to his long, hard body and kissed her as if he might never see her again. She pressed closer, wrapping her arms around him, holding on for dear life.

His mouth tasted of coffee. It was warm and hard, insistent as it ground into hers. She thought if she died now, it would be all right. She'd never been so happy.

She heard a soft groan from his mouth. One lean hand swept down her back and pressed her hips firmly into his. She stiffened a little. She didn't know much about men, but she was a great reader. The contours of his body had changed quite suddenly.

"Nothing to worry about," he whispered into her mouth. "Just relax . . ."

She did. It was intoxicating. His free hand went under her blouse and expertly unclasped her bra to give free rein to his searching fingers. They found her breast and teased the nipple until it went hard. He groaned and bent his head, putting his mouth right over it, over the cloth. She arched up to him, so entranced that she couldn't even find means to protest.

"Yes," he groaned. "Yes, yes . . . !"

Her hands tangled in his thick black hair, tugging it closer. She arched backward, held by his strong arms as he fed on the softness of her breast under his demanding mouth. His hand at her back was more insistent now, grinding her against the growing hardness of his body.

She was melting, dying, starving to death. She wanted him to take off her clothes; she wanted to lie down with him and she wanted something, anything that would ease the terrible ache in her young body.

And just when she was certain that it would happen, that he wasn't going to stop, a noisy car pulled into the car park above and a car door slammed.

She jerked back from him, tugging down her blouse, shivering at the interruption. His eyes were almost black with hunger. He cursed under his breath, biting his lip as he fought down the need that almost bent him over double.

From above there were children's voices, laughing and calling to each other. Maddie stood with her back to him, her arms wrapped around her body, while she struggled with wild excitement, embarrassment and confusion. He didn't like her. He thought she was ugly. But he'd kissed her as if he were dying for her mouth. It was one big puzzle . . .

She felt his big, warm hands on her shoulders. "Don't sweat it," he said in a deep, soft tone. "Things happen."

She swallowed and forced a smile. "Right."

He turned her around, tipping her red face up to his eyes. He searched them in a silence punctuated with the screams and laughter of children. She was very pretty like that, her mouth swollen from his kisses, her face shy, timid. He was used to women who demanded. Aggressive women. Even Odalie, when he'd kissed her once, had been very outspoken about what she liked and didn't like. Maddie simply . . . accepted.

"Don't be embarrassed," he said softly. "Everything's all right. But we should probably go now. It's getting late."

She nodded. He took her small hand in his, curled his fingers into hers and drew her with him along the dirt path that led back up to the parking lot.

Two bedraggled parents were trying to put out

food in plastic containers on a picnic table, fighting the wind, which was blowing like crazy in the sweltering heat. They glanced at the couple and grinned.

Cort grinned back. There were three children, all under school age, one in his father's arms. They looked happy, even though they were driving a car that looked as if it wouldn't make it out of the parking lot.

"Nice day for a picnic," Cort remarked.

The father made a face. "Not so much, but we've got a long drive ahead of us and it's hard to sit in a fast-food joint with this company." He indicated the leaping, running toddlers. He laughed. "Tomorrow, they'll be hijacking my car," he added with an ear-to-ear smile, "so we're enjoying it while we can."

"Nothing like kids to make a home a home," the mother commented.

"Nice looking kids, too," Cort said.

"Very nice," Maddie said, finally finding her voice.

"Thanks," the mother said. "They're a handful, but we don't mind."

She went back to her food containers, and the father went running after the toddlers, who were about to climb down the bank.

"Nice family," Cort remarked as they reached his car.

"Yes. They seemed so happy."

He glanced down at her as he stopped to open the passenger door. He was thoughtful. He didn't say anything, but his eyes were soft and full of secrets. "In you go."

She got in, fastened her seat belt without any prompting and smiled all the way back home.

Things were going great, until they got out of the car in front of Maddie's house. Pumpkin had found a way out of the hen enclosure. He spotted Cort and broke into a halting run, with his head down and his feathers ruffled.

"No!" Maddie yelled. "Pumpkin, no!"

She tried to head him off, but he jumped at her and she turned away just in time to avoid spurs in her face. "Cort, run! It's okay, just run!" she called when he hesitated.

He threw his hands up and darted toward his car. "You have to do something about that damned rooster, Maddie!" he called back.

"I know," she wailed. "I will, honest! I had fun. Thanks so much!"

He threw up his hands and dived into the car. He started it and drove off just before Pumpkin reached him.

"You stupid chicken! I'm going to let Ben eat you, I swear I am!" she raged.

But when he started toward her, she ran up the steps, into the house and slammed the door.

She opened her cell phone and called her foreman.

"Ben, can you please get Pumpkin back into the hen lot and try to see where he got out? Be sure to wear your chaps and carry a shield," she added.

"Need to eat that rooster, Maddie," he drawled.

"I know." She groaned. "Please?"

There was a long sigh. "All right. One more time . . ." He hung up.

Great-Aunt Sadie gave her a long look. "Pumpkin got out again?"

"Yes. There must be a hole in the fence or something," she moaned. "I don't know how in the world he does it!"

"Ben will find a way to shut him in, don't worry. But you are going to have to do something, you know. He's dangerous."

"I love him," Maddie said miserably.

"Well, sometimes things we love don't love us back and should be made into chicken and dumplings," Sadie mused with pursed lips.

Maddie made a face at her. She opened her shoulder bag and pulled out a box. "I want to show you something. Cort bought it for me."

"Cort's buying you presents?" Sadie exclaimed.

"It's some present, too," Maddie said with a flushed smile.

She opened the box. There, inside, was the hand-painted cameo of the little Spanish lady, with a card that gave all the information about the woman, now deceased, who left it with the antiques dealer.

"She's lovely," Sadie said, tracing the face with a forefinger very gently.

"Read the card." Maddie showed it to her.

When Sadie finished reading it, she was almost in tears. "How sad, to be the last one in your family."

"Yes. But this will be handed down someday." She was remembering the family at the picnic tables and Cort's strange smile, holding hands with him, kissing him. "Someday," she said again, and she sounded as breathless as she felt.

Sadie didn't ask any questions. But she didn't have to. Maddie's bemused expression told her everything she needed to know. Apparently Maddie and Cort were getting along very well, all of a sudden.

Cort walked into the house muttering about the rooster.

"Trouble again?" Shelby asked. She was curled up on the sofa watching the news, but she turned off the television when she saw her son. She smiled, dark-eyed and still beautiful.

"The rooster," he sighed. He tossed his hat into a chair and dropped down into his father's big recliner. "I bought us a bull. He's very nice."

"From Cy Parks?"

He nodded. "He's quite a character."

"So I've heard."

"I bought Maddie a cameo," he added. "In that tearoom halfway between here and Jacobsville. It's got an antiques store in with it." He shook his head. "Beautiful thing. It's hand-painted . . . a pretty Spanish lady with a fan, enameled. She had a fit over it. The seller died recently and had no family."

"Sad. But it was nice of you to buy it for Maddie."

He pursed his lips. "When you met Dad, you said you didn't get along."

She shivered dramatically. "That's putting it mildly. He hated me. Or he seemed to. But when my mother, your grandmother, died, I was alone in a media circus. They think she committed suicide and she was a big-name movie star, you see. So there was a lot of publicity. I was almost in hysterics when your father showed up out of nowhere and managed everything."

"Well!"

"I was shocked. He'd sent me home, told me he had a girlfriend and broke me up with Danny. Not that I needed breaking-up, Danny was only pretending to be engaged to me to make King face how he really felt. But it was fireworks from the start." She peered at him through her thick black eyelashes. "Sort of the way it was with you and Maddie, I think."

"It's fireworks, now, too. But of a different sort," he added very slowly.

"Oh?" She didn't want to pry, but she was curious.

"I'm confused. Maddie isn't pretty. She can't sing or play anything. But she can paint and sculpt and she's sharp about people." He grimaced. "Odalie is beautiful, like the rising sun, and she can play any instrument and sing like an angel."

"Accomplishments and education don't matter as much as personality and character," his mother replied quietly. "I'm not an educated person, although I've taken online courses. I made my living modeling. Do you think I'm less valuable to your father than a woman with a college degree and greater beauty?"

"Goodness, no!" he exclaimed at once.

She smiled gently. "See what I mean?"

"I think I'm beginning to." He leaned back. "It was a good day."

"I'm glad."

"Except for that damned rooster," he muttered. "One of these days . . . !"

She laughed.

He was about to call Maddie, just to talk, when his cell phone rang.

He didn't recognize the number. He put it up to his ear. "Hello?"

"Hello, Cort," Odalie's voice purred in his ear.

"Guess what, I'm home! Want to come over for supper tonight?"

He hesitated. Things had just gotten complicated.

Maddie half expected Cort to phone her, after their lovely day together, but he didn't. The next morning, she heard a car pull up in the driveway and went running out. But it wasn't Cort. It was John Everett.

She tried not to let her disappointment show. "Hi!" she said. "Would you like a cup of very nice European coffee from a fancy European coffee-maker?" she added, grinning.

He burst out laughing. "I would. Thanks. It's been a hectic day and night."

"Has it? Why?" she asked as they walked up the steps.

"I had to drive up to Dallas-Fort Worth airport to pick up Odalie yesterday."

Her heart did a nosedive. She'd hoped against hope that the other woman would stay in Italy, marry her voice teacher, get a job at the opera house, anything but come home, and especially right now! She and Cort were only just beginning to get to know each other. It wasn't fair!

"How is she?" she asked, her heart shattering.

"Good," he said heavily. "She and the voice teacher disagreed, so she's going to find someone in this country to take over from him."

He grimaced. "I don't know who. Since she knows more than the voice trainers do, I don't really see the point in it. She can't take criticism."

She swallowed, hard, as she went to work at the coffee machine. "Has Cort seen her?"

"Oh, yes," he said, sitting down at the little kitchen table. "He came over for supper last night. They went driving."

She froze at the counter. She didn't let him see her face, but her stiff back was a good indication of how she'd received the news.

"I'm really sorry," he said gently. "But I thought you should know before you heard gossip."

She nodded. Tears were stinging her eyes, but she hid them. "Thanks, John."

He drew in a long breath. "She doesn't love him," he said. "He's just a habit she can't give up. I don't think he loves her, either, really. It's like those crushes we get on movie stars. Odalie is an image, not someone real who wants to settle down and have kids and live on a ranch. She can't stand cattle!"

She started the coffee machine, collected herself, smiled and turned around. "Good thing your parents don't mind them," she said.

"And I've told her so. Repeatedly." He studied her through narrowed eyes. His thick blond hair shone like pale yellow diamonds in the overhead light. He was so good-looking, she thought. She wished she could feel for him what she felt for Cort.

"People can't help being who they are," she replied quietly.

"You're wise for your years," he teased.

She laughed. "Not so wise, or I'd get out of the cattle business." She chuckled. "After we have coffee, want to have another go at explaining genetics to me? I'm a lost cause, but we can try."

"You're not a lost cause, and I'd love to try."

Odalie was irritable and not trying to hide it. "What's the matter with you?" she snapped at Cort. "You haven't heard a word I've said."

He glanced at her and grimaced. "Sorry. We've got a new bull coming. I'm distracted."

Her pale blue eyes narrowed. "More than distracted, I think. What's this I hear about you taking that Lane girl with you to buy the new bull?"

He gave her a long look and didn't reply.

She cleared her throat. Cort was usually running after her, doing everything he could to make her happy, make her smile. She'd come home to find a stranger, a man she didn't know. Her beauty hadn't interested the voice trainer; her voice hadn't really impressed him. She'd come home with a damaged ego and wanted Cort to fix it by catering to her. That hadn't happened. She'd invited him over today for lunch and he'd eaten it in a fog. He actually seemed to not want to be with her, and that was new and scary.

"Well, she's plain as toast," Odalie said haughtily. "She has no talent and she's not educated."

He cocked his head. "And you think those are the most important character traits?"

She didn't like the way he was looking at her. "None of my friends had anything to do with her in school," she muttered.

"You had plenty to do with that, didn't you?" Cort asked with a cold smile. "I believe attorneys were involved . . . ?"

"Cort!" She went flaming red. She turned her head. "That was a terrible misunderstanding. And it was Millie who put me up to it. That's the truth. I didn't like Maddie, but I'd never have done it if I'd realized what that boy might do." She bit her lip. She'd thought about that a lot in recent weeks, she didn't know why. "He could have killed her. I'd have had it on my conscience forever," she added in a strange, absent tone.

Cort was not impressed. This was the first time he'd heard Odalie say anything about the other woman that didn't have a barb in it, and even this comment was self-centered. Though it was small, he still took her words as a sign that maybe she was changing and becoming more tolerant . . .

"Deep thoughts," he told her.

She glanced at him and smiled. "Yes. I've become introspective. Enjoy it while it lasts." She laughed, and she was so beautiful that he was really confused.

"I love your car," she said, glancing out the window. "Would you let me drive it?"

He hesitated. She was the worst driver he'd ever known. "As long as I'm in it," he said firmly.

She laughed. "I didn't mean I wanted to go alone," she teased.

She knew where she wanted to drive it, too. Right past Maddie Lane's house, so that she'd see Odalie with Cort. So she'd know that he was no longer available. Odalie seemed to have lost her chance at a career in opera, but here was Cort, who'd always loved her. Maybe she'd settle down, maybe she wouldn't, but Cort was hers. She wanted Maddie to know it.

She'd never driven a Jaguar before. This was a very fast, very powerful, very expensive two-seater. Cort handed her the key.

She clicked it to open the door. She frowned. "Where's the key?" she asked.

"You don't need a key. It's a smart key. You just keep it in your pocket or lay it in the cup holder."

"Oh."

She climbed into the car and put the smart key in the cup holder.

"Seat belt," he emphasized.

She glared at him. "It will wrinkle my dress," she said fussily, because it was delicate silk, pink and very pretty.

"Seat belt or the car doesn't move," he repeated.

She sighed. He was very forceful. She liked that. She smiled at him prettily. "Okay."

She put it on, grimacing as it wrinkled the delicate fabric. Oh, well, the dry cleaners could fix it. She didn't want to make Cort mad. She pushed the button Cort showed her, the button that would start the car, but nothing happened.

"Brake," he said.

She glared at him. "I'm not going fast enough to brake!"

"You have to put your foot on the brake or it won't start," he explained patiently.

"Oh."

She put her foot on the brake and it started. The air vents opened and the touch screen came on. "It's like something out of a science-fiction movie," she said, impressed.

"Isn't it, though?" He chuckled.

She glanced at him, her face radiant. "I have got to have Daddy get me one of these!" she exclaimed.

Cort hoped her father wouldn't murder him when he saw what they cost.

Odalie pulled the car out of the driveway in short jerks. She grimaced. "I haven't driven in a while, but it will come back to me, honest."

"Okay. I'm not worried." He was petrified, but he wasn't showing it. He hoped he could grab the wheel if he had to.

She smoothed out the motions when she got onto the highway. "There, better?" she teased, looking at him.

"Eyes on the road," he cautioned.

She sighed. "Cort, you're no fun."

"It's a powerful machine. You have to respect it. That means keeping your eyes on the road and paying attention to your surroundings."

"I'm doing that," she argued, looking at him again.

He prayed silently that they'd get home again.

She pulled off on a side road and he began to worry.

"Why are we going this way?" he asked suspiciously.

"Isn't this the way to Catelow?" she asked in all innocence.

"No, it's not," he said. "It's the road that leads to the Lane ranch."

"Oh, dear, I don't want to go there. But there's no place to turn off," she worried. "Anyway, the ranch is just ahead, I'll turn around there."

Cort had to bite his lip to keep from saying something.

Maddie was out in the yard with her garbage can lid. This time Pumpkin had gotten out of the pen when she was looking. He'd jumped a seven-foot-high fence. If she hadn't seen it with her own eyes, she'd never have believed it.

"Pumpkin, you fool!" she yelled at him. "Why can't you stay where I put you? Get back in there!"

But he ran around her. This time he wasn't even trying to spur her. He ran toward the road. It was his favorite place, for some reason, despite the heat that made the ribbon of black asphalt hotter than a frying pan.

"You come back here!" she yelled.

Just as she started after him, Odalie's foot hit the accelerator pedal too hard, Cort called out, Odalie looked at him instead of the road . . .

Maddie heard screaming. She was numb. She opened her eyes and there was Cort, his face contorted with horror. Beside him, Odalie was screaming and crying.

"Just lie still," Cort said hoarsely. "The ambulance is on the way. Just lie still, baby."

"I hit her, I hit her!" Odalie screamed. "I didn't see her until it was too late! I hit her!"

"Odalie, you have to calm down. You're not helping!" Cort snapped at her. "Find something to cover her. Hurry!"

"Yes . . . there's a blanket . . . in the backseat, isn't there . . . ?"

Odalie fetched it with cold, shaking hands. She drew it over Maddie's prone body. There was blood. So much blood. She felt as if she were going to faint, or throw up. Then she saw Maddie's face and tears ran down her cheeks. "Oh, Maddie," she sobbed, "I'm so sorry!"

"Find something to prop her head, in case her spine is injured," Cort gritted. He was terrified. He brushed back Maddie's blond hair, listened to her ragged breathing, saw her face go even paler. "Please hurry!" he groaned.

There wasn't anything. Odalie put her beautiful white leather purse on one side of Maddie's head without a single word, knowing it would ruin the leather and not caring at all. She put her knit overblouse on the other, crumpled up. She knelt in the dirt road beside Maddie and sat down, tears in her eyes. She touched Maddie's arm. "Help is coming," she whispered brokenly. "You hold on, Maddie. Hold on!"

Maddie couldn't believe it. Her worst enemy was sitting beside her in a vision of a horrifically expensive pink silk dress that was going to be absolutely ruined, and apparently didn't mind at all.

She tried to speak. "Pum . . . Pumpkin?" she rasped.

Cort looked past her and grimaced. He didn't say anything. He didn't have to.

Maddie started to cry, great heaving sobs.

"We'll get you another rooster," Cort said at once. "I'll train him to attack me. Anything. You just have to . . . hold on, baby," he pleaded. "Hold on!"

She couldn't breathe. "Hurts," she whispered as sensation rushed back in and she began to shudder.

Cort was in hell. There was no other word that would express what he felt as he saw her lying there in bloody clothing, maybe dying, and he couldn't do one damned thing to help her. He was sick to his soul.

He brushed back her hair, trying to remember anything else, anything that would help her until the ambulance arrived.

"Call them again!" Odalie said firmly.

He did. The operator assured them that the ambulance was almost there. She began asking questions, which Cort did his best to answer.

"Where's your great-aunt?" he asked Maddie softly.

"Store," she choked out.

"It's okay, I'll call her," he said when she looked upset.

Odalie had come out of her stupor and she was checking for injuries while Cort talked to the 911 operator. "I don't see anything that looks dangerous, but I'm afraid to move her," she said, ignoring the blood in her efforts to give aid. "There are some abrasions, pretty raw ones. Maddie, can you move your arms and legs?" she asked in a voice so tender that Maddie thought maybe she really was just dreaming all this.

She moved. "Yes," she said. "But . . . it hurts . . ."

"Move your ankles."

"Okay."

Odalie looked at Cort with horror.

"I moved . . . them," Maddie said, wincing. "Hurts!"

"Please, ask them to hurry," Cort groaned into the phone.

"No need," Odalie said, noting the red-and-white vehicle that was speeding toward them.

"No sirens?" Cort asked blankly.

"They don't run the sirens or lights unless they have to," the operator explained kindly. "It scares people to death and can cause wrecks. They'll use them to get the victim to the hospital, though, you bet," she reassured him.

"Thanks so much," Cort said.

"I hope she does well."

"Me, too," he replied huskily and hung up.

Odalie took one of the EMTs aside. "She can't move her feet," she whispered.

He nodded. "We won't let her know."

They went to the patient.

Maddie wasn't aware of anything after they loaded her into the ambulance on a backboard. They talked to someone on the radio and stuck a needle into her arm. She slept.

When she woke again, she was in a hospital bed

with two people hovering. Cort and Odalie. Odalie's dress was dirty and bloodstained.

"Your . . . beautiful dress," Maddie whispered, wincing.

Odalie went to the bed. She felt very strange. Her whole life she'd lived as if there was nobody else around. She'd never been in the position of nursing anybody—her parents and brother had never even sprained a hand. She'd been petted, spoiled, praised, but never depended upon.

Now here was this woman, this enemy, whom her actions had placed almost at death's door. And suddenly she was needed. Really needed.

Maddie's great-aunt had been called. She was in the waiting room, but in no condition to be let near the patient. The hospital staff had to calm her down, she was so terrified.

They hadn't told Maddie yet. When Sadie was calmer, they'd let her in to see the injured woman.

"Your great-aunt is here, too," Odalie said gently. "You're going to be fine."

"Fine." Maddie felt tears run down her cheeks. "So much . . . to be done at the ranch, and I'm stove up . . . !"

"I'll handle it," Cort said firmly. "No worries there."

"Pumpkin," she sobbed. "He was horrible. Just horrible. But I loved him." She cried harder.

Odalie leaned down and kissed her unkempt

hair. "We'll find you another horrible rooster. Honest."

Maddie sobbed. "You hate me."

"No," Odalie said softly. "No, I don't. And I'm so sorry that I put you in here. I was driving." She bit her lip. "I wasn't watching the road," she said stiffly. "God, I'm sorry!"

Maddie reached out a lacerated hand and touched Odalie's. "I ran into the road after Pumpkin . . . I wasn't looking. Not your fault. My fault."

Odalie was crying, too. "Okay. Both our faults. Now we have to get you well."

"Both of us," Cort agreed, touching Maddie's bruised cheek.

Maddie swallowed, hard. She wanted to say something else, but they'd given her drugs to make her comfortable, apparently. She opened her mouth to speak and went right to sleep.

Chapter Seven

"Is she going to be all right?" Great-Aunt Sadie asked when Odalie and Cort dropped into chairs in the waiting room while Maddie was sleeping.

"Yes, but it's going to be a long recovery," Cort said heavily.

"You can't tell her," Odalie said gently, "but there seems to be some paralysis in her legs. No, it's all right," she interrupted when Sadie looked as if she might start crying. "We've called one of the foremost orthopedic surgeons in the country at the Mayo Clinic. We're flying him down here to see her. We'll go from there, once he's examined her."

"But the expense," Sadie exclaimed.

"No expense. None. This is my fault and I'm paying for it," Odalie said firmly.

"It's my car, I'm helping," Cort added.

She started crying again. "It's so nice of you, both of you."

Odalie hugged her. "I'm so sorry," she said sadly. "I didn't mean to hit her. I wasn't looking, and I should have been."

Sadie hugged her back. "Accidents happen," she sobbed. "It was that stupid rooster, wasn't it?"

"It was." Cort sighed. "He ran right into the road and Maddie ran after him. The road was clear and then, seconds later, she was in the middle of it."

Odalie couldn't confess that she'd gone that way deliberately to show Maddie she was with Cort. She was too ashamed. "She'll be all right," she promised.

"Oh, my poor little girl," Sadie said miserably. "She'll give up, if she knows she might not be able to walk again. She won't fight!"

"She will. Because we'll make her," Odalie said quietly.

Sadie looked at her with new eyes. Her gaze fell to Odalie's dress. "Oh, your dress," she exclaimed.

Odalie just smiled. "I can get another dress. It's Maddie I'm worried about." It sounded like a glib reply, but it wasn't. In the past few hours, Odalie's outlook had totally shifted from herself to someone who needed her. She knew that her life would never be the same again.

A sheriff's deputy came into the waiting room, spotted Odalie and Cort and approached them, shaking his head.

"I know," Odalie said. "It's my fault. I was driving his car—" she indicated Cort "—and not looking where I was going. Maddie ran out into the road after her stupid rooster, trying to save him. She's like that."

The deputy smiled. "We know all that from the re-creation of the scene that we did," he said. "It's very scientific," he added. "How is she?"

"Bad," Odalie said heavily. "They think she may lose the use of her legs. But we've called in a world-famous surgeon. If anything can be done, it will be. We're going to take care of her."

The deputy looked at the beautiful woman, at her bloodstained, dirty, expensive dress, with kind eyes. "I know some women who would be much more concerned with the state of their clothing than the state of the victim. Your parents must be very proud of you, young lady. If you were my daughter, I would be."

Odalie flushed and smiled. "I feel pretty guilty right now. So thanks for making me feel better."

"You going to charge her?" Cort asked.

The deputy shook his head. "Probably not, as long as she survives. In the law, everything is intent. You didn't mean to do it, and the young lady ran into the road by her own admission." He didn't add that having to watch the results of the accident day after day would probably be a worse punishment than anything the law could prescribe. But he was thinking it.

"That doesn't preclude the young lady pressing charges, however," the deputy added.

Odalie smiled wanly. "I wouldn't blame her if she did."

He smiled back. "I hope she does well."

"So do we," Odalie agreed. "Thanks."

He nodded and went back out again.

"Tell me what the doctor said about her legs," Sadie said sadly, leaning toward them.

Odalie took a long breath. She was very tired and she had no plans to go home that night. She'd have to call her family and tell them what was happening here. She hadn't had time to do that yet, nor had Cort.

"He said that there's a great deal of bruising, with inflammation and swelling. That can cause partial paralysis, apparently. He's started her on anti-inflammatories and when she's able, he'll have her in rehab to help get her moving," she added gently.

"But she was in so much pain . . . surely they won't make her get up!" Sadie was astonished.

"The longer she stays there, the stronger the possibility that she won't ever get up, Sadie," Odalie said gently. She patted the other woman's hands, which were resting clenched in her lap. "He's a very good doctor."

"Yes," Sadie said absently. "He treated my nephew when he had cancer. Sent him to some of the best oncologists in Texas." She looked up. "So maybe it isn't going to be permanent?"

"A good chance. So you stop worrying. We all have to be strong so that we can make her look ahead instead of behind, so that we can keep her from brooding." She bit her lower lip. "It's going to be very depressing for her, and it's going to be a long haul, even if it has a good result."

"I don't care. I'm just so happy she's still alive," the older woman cried.

"Oh, so am I," Odalie said heavily. "I can't remember ever feeling quite so bad in all my life. I took my eyes off the road, just for a minute." Her eyes closed and she shuddered. "I'll be able to hear that horrible sound when I'm an old lady . . ."

Cort put his arm around her. "Stop that. I shouldn't have let you drive the car until you were familiar with it. My fault, too. I feel as bad as you do. But we're going to get Maddie back on her feet."

"Yes," Odalie agreed, forcing a smile. "Yes, we are."

Sadie wiped her eyes and looked from one young determined face to the other. Funny how things worked out, she was thinking. Here was Odalie, Maddie's worst enemy, being protective of her, and Cort just as determined to make her walk again when he'd been yelling at her only a week or so earlier. What odd companions they were going to be for her young great-niece. But what a blessing.

She considered how it could have worked out, if Maddie had chased that stupid red rooster out into the road and been hit by someone else, maybe someone who ran and left her there to die. It did happen. The newspapers were full of such cases.

"What are you thinking so hard about?" Cort asked with a faint smile.

Sadie laughed self-consciously. "That if she had to get run over, it was by such nice people who stopped and rendered aid."

"I know what you mean," Cort replied. "A man was killed just a couple of weeks ago by a hit-and-run driver who was drunk and took off. The pedestrian died. I wondered at the time if his life might have been spared, if the man had just stopped to call an ambulance before he ran." He shook his head. "So many cases like that."

"Well, you didn't run, either of you." Sadie smiled. "Thanks, for saving my baby."

Odalie hugged her again, impulsively. "For the foreseeable future, she's my baby, too," she said with a laugh. "Now, how about some coffee? I don't know about you, but I'm about to go to sleep out here and I have no intention of leaving the hospital."

"Nor do I," Cort agreed. He stood up. "Let's go down to the cafeteria and see what we can find to eat, too. I just realized I'm starving."

The women smiled, as they were meant to.

Maddie came around a long time later, or so it seemed. A dignified man with black wavy hair was standing over her with a nurse. He was wearing a white lab coat with a stethoscope draped around his neck.

"Miss Lane?" the nurse asked gently. She smiled. "This is Dr. Parker from the Mayo Clinic. He's an orthopedic specialist, and we'd like him to have a look at your back. If you don't mind."

Maddie cleared her throat. She didn't seem to be in pain, which was odd. She felt very drowsy. "Of course," she said, puzzled as to why they would have such a famous man at such a small rural hospital.

"Just a few questions first," he said in a deep, pleasant tone, "and then I'll examine you." He smiled down at her.

"Okay."

The pain came back as the examination progressed, but he said it was a good sign. Especially the pain she felt in one leg. He pressed and poked and asked questions while he did it. After a few minutes she was allowed to lie down in the bed, which she did with a grimace of pure relief.

"There's a great deal of edema—swelling," he translated quietly. "Bruising of the spinal column, inflammation, all to be expected from the trauma you experienced."

"I can't feel my legs. I can't move them," Maddie said with anguish in her wan face.

He dropped down elegantly into the chair by her bed, crossed his legs and picked up her chart. "Yes, I know. But you mustn't give up hope. I have every confidence that you'll start to regain feeling in a couple of weeks, three at the outside. You have to believe that as well." He made notations and read what her attending physician had written in the forms on the clipboard, very intent on every word. "He's started you on anti-inflammatories," he murmured. "Good, good, just what I would have advised. Getting fluids into you intravenously, antibiotics . . ." He stopped and made another notation. "And then, physical therapy."

"Physical therapy." She laughed and almost cried. "I can't stand up!"

"It's much more than just exercise," he said

and smiled gently. "Heat, massage, gentle movements, you'll see. You've never had physical therapy I see."

She shook her head. "I've never really had an injury that required it."

"You're very lucky, then," he said.

"You think I'll walk again?" she prompted, her eyes wide and full of fear.

"I think so," he said. "I won't lie to you, there's a possibility that the injury may result in permanent disability." He held up a hand when she seemed distraught. "If that happens, you have a wonderful support group here. Your family. They'll make sure you have everything you need. You'll cope. You'll learn how to adapt. I've seen some miraculous things in my career, Miss Lane," he added. "One of my newest patients lost a leg overseas in a bombing. We repaired the damage, got him a prosthesis and now he's playing basketball."

She caught her breath. "Basketball?"

He grinned, looking much younger. "You'd be amazed at the advances science has made in such things. Right now, they're working on an interface that will allow quadriplegics to use a computer with just thought. Sounds like science fiction, doesn't it? But it's real. I watched a video of a researcher who linked a man's mind electronically to a computer screen, and he was able to move a curser just with the power of his thoughts." He shook his head. "Give those guys ten years and they'll build something that can read minds."

"Truly fascinating," she agreed.

"But right now, what I want from you is a promise that you'll do what your doctor tells you and work hard at getting back on your feet," he said. "No brooding. No pessimism. You have to believe you'll walk again."

She swallowed. She was bruised and broken and miserable. She drew in a breath. "I'll try," she said.

He stood up and handed the chart to the nurse with a smile. "I'll settle for that, as long as it's your very best try," he promised. He shook hands with her. "I'm going to stay in touch with your doctor and be available for consultation. If I'm needed, I can fly back down here. Your friends out there sent a private jet for me." He chuckled. "I felt like a rock star."

She laughed, then, for the first time since her ordeal had begun.

"That's more like it," he said. "Ninety-nine percent of recovery is in the mind. You remember that."

"I'll remember," she promised. "Thanks for coming all this way."

He threw up a hand. "Don't apologize for that. It got me out of a board meeting," he said. "I hate board meetings."

She grinned.

Later, after she'd been given her medicines and fed, Odalie and Cort came into the private room she'd been moved to.

"Dr. Parker is very nice," she told them. "He came all the way from the Mayo Clinic, though . . . !"

"Whatever it takes is what you'll get," Odalie said with a smile.

Maddie grimaced as she looked at Odalie's beautiful pink dress, creased and stained with blood and dirt. "Your dress," she moaned.

"I've got a dozen pretty much just like it," Odalie told her. "I won't even miss it." She sighed. "But I really should go home and change."

"Go home and go to bed," Maddie said softly. "You've done more than I ever expected already . . ."

"No," Odalie replied. "I'm staying with you. I got permission."

"But there's no bed," Maddie exclaimed. "You can't sleep in a chair . . . !"

"There's a rollaway bed. They're bringing it in." She glanced at Cort with a wicked smile. "Cort gets to sleep in the chair."

He made a face. "Don't rub it in."

"But you don't have to stay," Maddie tried to reason with them. "I have nurses. I'll be fine, honest I will."

Odalie moved to the bed and brushed Maddie's

unkempt hair away from her wan face. "You'll brood if we leave you alone," she said reasonably. "It's not as if I've got a full social calendar these days, and I'm not much for cocktail parties. I'd just as soon be here with you. We can talk about art. I majored in it at college."

"I remember," Maddie said slowly. "I don't go to college," she began.

"I'll wager you know more about it than I do," Odalie returned. "You had to learn something of anatomy to make those sculptures so accurate."

"Well, yes, I did," Maddie faltered. "I went on the internet and read everything I could find."

"I have all sorts of books on medieval legends and romances, I'll bring them over for you to read when they let you go home. Right now you have to rest," Odalie said.

Maddie flushed. "That would be so nice of you."

Odalie's eyes were sad. "I've been not so nice to you for most of the time we've known one another," she replied. "You can't imagine how I felt, after what happened because I let an idiot girl talk me into telling lies about you online. I've had to live with that, just as you have. I never even said I was sorry for it. But I am," she added.

Maddie drew in a breath. She was feeling drowsy. "Thanks," she said. "It means a lot."

"Don't you worry about a thing," Odalie added. "I'll take care of you."

Maddie flushed. She'd never even really had a girlfriend, and here was Odalie turning out to be one.

Odalie smiled. "Now go to sleep. Things will look brighter tomorrow. Sometimes a day can make all the difference in how we look at life."

"I'll try."

"Good girl." She glanced at Cort. "Can you drive me home and bring me back?"

"Sure," he said. "I need a change of clothes, too. I'll drop you off at Big Spur, go home and clean up and we'll both come back. We need to tell our parents what's going on, too."

"John will be beside himself," Odalie said without thinking. "All I've heard since I got home is how sweet Maddie is," she added with a smile.

She didn't see Cort's expression, and she couldn't understand why Maddie suddenly looked so miserable at the mention of her brother's name.

"Well, don't worry about that right now," Odalie said quickly. "But I'm sure he'll be in to see you as soon as he knows what happened."

Maddie nodded.

"I'll be right out," Cort said, smiling at Odalie.

"Sure. Sleep tight," she told Maddie. She hesitated. "I'm sorry about your rooster, too. Really sorry," she stammered, and left quickly.

Maddie felt tears running down her cheeks.

Cort picked a tissue out of the box by the bed,

bent down and dabbed at both her eyes. "Stop that," he said softly. "They'll think I'm pinching you and throw me out."

She smiled sadly. "Nobody would ever think you were mean."

"Don't you believe it."

"You and Odalie . . . you've both been so kind," she said hesitantly. "Thank you."

"We feel terrible," he replied, resting his hand beside her tousled hair on the pillow. "It could have been a worse tragedy than it is. And Pumpkin . . ." He grimaced and dabbed at more tears on her face. "As much as I hated him, I really am sorry. I know you loved him."

She sniffed, and he dabbed at her nose, too. "He was so mean," she choked out. "But I really did love him."

"We'll get you a new rooster. I'll train him to attack me," he promised.

She laughed through her tears.

"That's better. The way you looked just now was breaking my heart."

She searched his eyes. He wasn't joking. He meant it.

He brushed back her hair. "God, I don't know what I would have done if you'd died," he whispered hoarsely. He bent and crushed his mouth down over hers, ground into it with helpless need. After a few seconds, he forced himself to pull back. "Sorry," he said huskily.

"Couldn't help myself. I was terrified when I saw you lying there so still."

"You were?" She looked fascinated.

He shook his head and forced a smile. "Clueless," he murmured. "I guess that's not such a bad thing. Not for the moment anyway." He bent and brushed his mouth tenderly over hers. "I'll be back. Don't go anywhere."

"If I tried to, three nurses would tackle me, and a doctor would sit on me while they sent for a gurney," she assured him, her eyes twinkling.

He wrinkled his nose and kissed her again. "Okay." He stood up. "Anything you want me to bring you?"

"A steak dinner, two strawberry milkshakes, a large order of fries . . ."

"For that, they'd drag me out the front door and pin me to a wall with scalpels," he assured her.

She sighed. "Oh, well. It was worth a try. They fed me green gelatin." She made a face.

"When we get you out of here, I'll buy you the tastiest steak in Texas, and that's a promise. With fries."

"Ooooh," she murmured.

He grinned. "Incentive to get better. Yes?"

She nodded. "Yes." The smile faded. "You don't have to come back. Odalie, either. I'll be okay."

"We're coming back, just the same. We'll drop Great-Aunt Sadie off at the house, but she can stay at Skylance if she's nervous about being there alone. She's been a real trooper, but she's very upset."

"Can I see her?"

"For just a minute. I'll bring her in. You be good." She nodded.

Great-Aunt Sadie was still crying when she went to the bed and very carefully bent down to hug Maddie. "I'm so glad you're going to be all right," she sobbed.

Maddie touched her gray hair gently. "Can't kill a weed." She laughed.

"You're no weed, my baby." She smoothed back her hair. "You keep getting better. I'll bring your gown and robe and slippers and some cash when I come back. Here. This is for the machines if you want them to get you anything . . ."

"Put that back," Cort said, "Maddie won't need cash."

"Oh, but—" Sadie started to argue.

"It won't do any good," Cort interrupted with a grin. "Ask my dad."

"He's right," Maddie said drowsily. "I heard one of his cowboys say that it's easier to argue with a signpost, and you'll get further."

"Stop bad-mouthing me. Bad girl," he teased.

She grinned sleepily.

"You go to sleep," he told her. "Odalie and I will be back later, and we'll bring Sadie in the morning."

"You're a nice boy, Cort," Sadie said tearfully.

He hugged her. "You're a nice girl," he teased. "Good night, honey," he told Maddie, and didn't miss the faint blush in her cheeks as she registered the endearment.

"Good night," she replied.

She drifted off to sleep before they got out of the hospital. In her mind, she could still hear that soft, deep voice drawling "honey."

The next morning, Maddie opened her eyes when she heard a commotion.

"I can't bathe her with you sitting there," the nurse was saying reasonably.

Cort frowned as he stood up. "I know, I know. Sorry. I only fell asleep about four," he added with a sheepish smile.

The nurse smiled back. "It's all right. A lot of patients don't have anybody who even cares if they live or die. Your friend's very fortunate that the two of you care so much."

"She's a sweet girl," Odalie said gently.

"So are you," Cort said, and smiled warmly at her. She flushed a little.

Maddie, watching, felt her heart sink. They'd both been so caring and attentive that she'd actually forgotten how Cort felt about Odalie. And now it seemed that Odalie was seeing him with new eyes.

Cort turned, but Maddie closed her eyes. She couldn't deal with this. Not now.

"Tell her we went to have breakfast and we'll be back," Cort said, studying Maddie's relaxed face.

"I will," the nurse promised.

Cort let Odalie go out before him and closed the door as he left.

"Time to wake up, sweetie," the nurse told Maddie. "I'm going to give you your bath and then you can have breakfast."

"Oh, is it morning?" Maddie asked, and pretended to yawn. "I slept very well."

"Good. Your friends went to have breakfast. That handsome man said they'd be back," she added with a laugh. "And that woman. What I wouldn't give to be that beautiful!"

"She sings like an angel, too," Maddie said.

"My, my, as handsome as he is, can you imagine what beautiful children they'd have?" the nurse murmured as she got her things together to bathe Maddie.

"Yes, wouldn't they?" Maddie echoed.

Something in her tone made the other woman look at her curiously.

But Maddie just smiled wanly. "They've both been very kind," she said. "They're my neighbors."

"I see."

No, she didn't, but Maddie changed the subject to a popular television series that she watched. The nurse watched it, too, which gave them a talking point.

● ● ●

Later, Sadie came in with a small overnight bag.

"I brought all your stuff," she told Maddie. "You look better," she lied, because Maddie was pale and lethargic and obviously fighting pain.

"It's a little worse today," she replied heavily. "You know what they say about injuries, they're worse until the third day and then they start getting better."

"Who said that?" Sadie wondered.

"Beats me, but I've heard it all my life. Did you bring me anything to read?" she added curiously.

"I didn't. But somebody else did." She glanced at the door. Odalie came in with three beautifully illustrated fairy-tale books. After breakfast, both Odalie and Cort had gone home to change, and then picked up Great-Aunt Sadie when returning to the hospital.

"I bought these while I was in college," Odalie said, handing one to Maddie. "I thought they had some of the most exquisite plates I'd ever seen."

And by plates, she meant paintings. Maddie caught her breath as she opened the book and saw fairies, like the ones she made, depicted in a fantasy forest with a shimmering lake.

"Oh, this is . . . it's beyond words," she exclaimed, breathlessly turning pages.

"Yes. I thought you'd like them." She beamed. "These are updated versions of the ones I have. I bought these for you."

"For me?" Maddie looked as if she'd won the lottery. "You mean it?"

"I mean it. I'm so glad you like them."

"They're beautiful," she whispered reverently. She traced one of the fairies. "I have my own ideas about faces and expressions, but these are absolutely inspiring!"

"Fantasy art is my favorite."

"Mine, too." She looked up, flushing a little. "How can I ever thank you enough?"

"You can get better so that my conscience will stop killing me," Odalie said gently.

Maddie smiled. "Okay. I promise to try."

"I'll settle for that."

"I put your best gowns and slippers in the bag," Sadie told her. "And Cort brought you something, too."

"Cort?"

She looked toward the door. He was smiling and nodding at the nurses, backing into the room. Behind his back was a strange, bottom-heavy bear with a big grin and bushy eyebrows.

He turned into the room and handed it to Maddie. "I don't know if they'll let you keep it, but if they won't, I'll let Sadie take him home and put him in your room. His name's Bubba."

"Bubba?" She burst out laughing as she took the bear from him. It was the cutest stuffed bear she'd ever seen. "Oh, he's so cute!"

"I'm glad you like him. I wanted to smuggle

in a steak, but they'd have smelled it at the door."

"Thanks for the thought," she said shyly.

"You're welcome."

"Bears and books." She sighed. "I feel spoiled."

"I should hope so," Odalie said with a grin. "We're doing our best."

"When we get you out of here, we're taking you up to Dallas and we'll hit all the major museums and art galleries," Cort said, dropping into a chair. "Culture. Might give you some new ideas for your paintings and sculptures."

"Plus we bought out an art supply store for you," Odalie said with twinkling eyes. "You'll have enough to make all sorts of creations when you get home."

"Home." Maddie looked from one of them to the other. "When? When can I go home?"

"In a few days." Cort spoke for the others. "First they have to get you stabilized. Then you'll be on a regimen of medicine and physical therapy. We'll go from there."

Maddie drew in a long breath. It sounded like an ordeal. She wasn't looking forward to it. And afterward, what if she could never walk again? What if . . . ?

"No pessimistic thoughts." Odalie spoke for the visitors. "You're going to get well. You're going to walk. Period."

"Absolutely," Sadie said.

"Amen," Cort added.

Maddie managed a sheepish smile. With a cheering section like that, she thought, perhaps she could, after all.

Chapter Eight

The third day was definitely the worst. Maddie was in incredible pain from all the bruising. It was agony to move at all, and her legs were still numb. They kept her sedated most of the day. And at night, as usual, Cort and Odalie stayed with her.

"How are you getting away with this?" Maddie asked Odalie when Cort left to get them both a cup of coffee.

"With this?" Odalie asked gently.

"Staying in the room with me," she replied drowsily. "I thought hospitals made people leave at eight-thirty."

"Well, they mostly do," Odalie said sheepishly. "But, you see, Cort's Dad endowed the new pediatric unit, and mine paid for the equipment in the physical therapy unit. So, they sort of made an exception for us."

Maddie laughed in spite of the pain. "Oh, my."

"As my dad explained it, you can do a lot of

good for other people and help defray your own taxes, all at once. But, just between us, my dad would give away money even if it didn't help his tax bill. So would Cort's. It's just the sort of people they are."

"It's very nice of them." She shifted and grimaced. "How are things at my ranch, do you know?" she asked worriedly.

"Great. Not that the boys don't miss you. But Cort's been over there every day getting roundup organized and deciding on your breeding program. I hope you don't mind."

"Are you kidding? I make fairies . . . I don't know anything about creating bloodlines." She sighed. "My dad knew all that stuff. He was great at it. But he should have had a boy who'd have loved running a ranch. I just got stuck with it because there was nobody else he could leave it to."

"Your father must have known that you'd do the best you could to keep it going," Odalie said gently.

"I am. It's just I have no aptitude for it, that's all."

"I think . . ."

"Finally!" John Everett said as he walked in, frowning at his sister. "There was such a conspiracy of silence. I couldn't get Cort to tell me where you were. I called every hospital in Dallas . . ."

"I left you seven emails and ten text messages!" Odalie gasped. "Don't tell me you never read them?"

He glowered at her. "I don't read my personal email because it's always advertisements, and I hate text messages. I disabled them from coming to my phone. You couldn't have called me in Denver and told me what happened?"

Odalie would have told him that Cort talked her out of it, but he was mad, and John in a temper would discourage most people from confessing that.

"Sorry," she said instead.

He turned his attention to Maddie and grimaced. The bruises were visible around the short-sleeved gown she was wearing. "Poor little thing," he said gently. "I brought you flowers."

He opened the door and nodded to a lady standing outside with a huge square vase full of every flower known to man—or so it seemed. "Right over there looks like a good place," he said, indicating a side table.

The lady, probably from the gift shop, smiled at Maddie and placed the flowers on the table. "I hope you feel better soon," she told her.

"The flowers are just lovely," Maddie exclaimed.

"Thanks," the lady replied, smiled at John and left them to it.

"Oh, how beautiful. Thanks, John!" she exclaimed.

Odalie looked very uncomfortable. John didn't even look at her. He went to the bedside, removed his Stetson and sat down in the chair by the bed, grasping one of Maddie's hands in his. "I've been beside myself since I knew what happened. I wanted to fly right home, but I was in the middle of negotiations for Dad and I couldn't. I did try to call your house, but nobody answered, and I didn't have your cell phone number." He glared at his sister again. "Nobody would even tell me which hospital you were in!"

"I sent you emails," Odalie said again.

"The telephone has a voice mode," he drawled sarcastically.

Odalie swallowed hard and got to her feet. "Maybe I should help Cort carry the coffee," she said. "Do you want some?"

"Don't be mean to her," Maddie said firmly. "She's been wonderful to me."

John blinked. He glanced at Odalie with wide-eyed surprise. "Her?"

"Yes, her," Maddie replied. "She hasn't left me since I've been in here. She brought me books . . ."

"Her?" John exclaimed again.

Odalie glared at him. "I am not totally beyond redemption," she said haughtily.

"Maybe I have a fever," John mused, touching his forehead as he looked back down into

Maddie's eyes. "I thought you said she stayed with you in the hospital. She hates hospitals."

"She's been here all night every night," Maddie said softly. She smiled at Odalie. "She's been amazing."

Odalie went beet-red. She didn't know how to handle the compliment. She'd had so many, all her life, about her beauty and her talent. But nobody had ever said she was amazing for exhibiting compassion. It felt really good.

"It was my fault, what happened," Odalie said quietly. "I was driving."

"Who the hell let you drive a car?" John exclaimed.

"I did," Cort said heavily as he joined them. He looked at John's hand holding Maddie's and his dark eyes began to burn with irritation. "Don't hold her hand, it's bruised," he blurted out before he thought.

John's blue eyes twinkled suddenly. "It is?" He turned it over and looked at it. "Doesn't look bruised. That hurt?" he asked Maddie.

"Well, no," she answered. The way Cort was looking at John was very odd.

"Yes, he let me drive because I badgered him into it," Odalie broke in. "Poor Maddie tried to save her rooster and ran out into the road. I didn't see her until it was too late."

"Oh, no," John said, concerned. "Will you be all right?" he asked Maddie.

"I'm going to be fine," she assured him with more confidence than she really felt.

"Yes, she is," Odalie said, smiling. "We're all going to make sure of it."

"What about Pumpkin?" John asked.

Odalie tried to stop him from asking, but she was too late.

"It's all right," Maddie said gently. "I'm getting used to it. Pumpkin . . . didn't make it."

Sadie had told her that Ben had buried the awful rooster under a mesquite tree and even made a little headstone to go on the grave. Considering how many scars Ben had, it was quite a feat of compassion.

"I'll get you a new rooster," John said firmly.

"Already taken care of," Cort replied. "You're in my seat, bro."

John gave him a strange look. "Excuse me?"

"That's my seat. I've got it just the way I like it, from sleeping in it for two nights."

John was getting the picture. He laughed inside. Amazing how determined Cort was to get him away from Maddie. He glanced at his sister, who should be fuming. But she wasn't. Her eyes were smiling. She didn't even seem to be jealous.

Maddie was so out of it that she barely noticed the byplay. The sedative was working on her. She could barely keep her eyes open.

As she drifted off, Cort was saying something about a rooster with feathers on his feet. . . .

A week after the accident, Maddie began to feel her back again. It was agonizing pain. Dr. Brooks came in to examine her, his face impassive as he had her grip his fingers. He used a pin on the bottom of her feet, and actually grinned when she flinched.

"I'm not going to be paralyzed?" she asked, excited and hopeful.

"We can't say that for sure," Dr. Brooks said gently. "Once the swelling and edema are reduced, there may be additional injuries that become apparent. But I will say it's a good sign."

She let out a breath. "I'd have coped," she assured him. "But I'm hoping I won't have to."

He smiled and patted her on the shoulder. "One step at a time, young lady. Recovery first, then rehabilitation with physiotherapy. Meanwhile I'm going to consult with your orthopedic surgeon and put in a call to a friend of mine, a neurologist. We want to cover all our bases."

"You're being very cautious," she murmured.

"I have to be. The fact that you got excellent immediate care at the scene is greatly in your favor, however. Cort knew exactly what to do, and the paramedics followed up in textbook perfection. However," he added with a smile, "my personal opinion is your condition comes from bad bruising and it is not a permanent injury. We saw nothing on the tests that indicated a tearing of the spinal cord or critical damage to any of your lumbar vertebrae."

"You didn't say," she replied.

"Until the swelling goes down, we can't be absolutely sure of anything, which is why I'm reluctant to go all bright-eyed over a cheery prognosis," he explained. "But on the evidence of what I see, I think you're going to make a complete recovery."

She beamed. "Thank you!"

He held up a hand. "We'll still wait and see."

"When can I go home?" she asked.

"Ask me next week."

She made a face. "I'm tired of colored gelatin," she complained. "They're force feeding me water and stuff with fiber in it."

"To keep your kidney and bowel function within acceptable levels," he said. "Don't fuss. Do what they tell you."

She sighed. "Okay. Thanks for letting Cort and Odalie stay with me at night. One of the nurses said you spoke to the administrator himself."

He shrugged. "He and I were at med school together. I beat him at chess regularly."

She laughed. "Can you thank him for me? You don't know what it meant, that they wanted to stay."

"Yes, I do," he replied solemnly. "I've never

seen anybody do a greater turnaround than your friend Odalie." He was the doctor who'd treated Maddie after the boy tried to throw her out of the window at school. He'd given a statement to the attorneys who went to see Cole Everett, as well. He shook his head. "I've known your families since you were children. I know more about Odalie than most people do. I must say, she's impressed me. And I'm hard to impress."

Maddie smiled. "She's impressed me, too. I never expected her to be so compassionate. Of course, it could be guilt," she said hesitantly. She didn't add that Odalie could be trying to win back Cort. She made a face. "I'm ashamed that I said that."

"Don't be. It's natural to be suspicious of someone who's been nothing short of an enemy. But this time, I believe her motives are quite sincere."

"Thanks. That helps."

He smiled. "You keep improving. I'll be back to see you from time to time. But I'm pleased with the progress I see."

"Thanks more for that."

He chuckled. "I love my job," he said at the door.

Late at night, Maddie was prey to her secret fears of losing the use of her legs. Despite Dr. Brooks's assurances, she knew that the prognosis could change. The traumatic nature of her injury made it unpredictable.

"Hey," Cort said softly, holding her hand when she moved restlessly in bed. "Don't think about tomorrow. Just get through one day at a time."

She rolled her head on the pillow and looked at him with tormented eyes. Odalie was sound asleep on the rollaway bed nearby, oblivious. But last night, it had been the other woman who'd been awake while Cort slept, to make sure Maddie had anything she needed.

"It's hard not to think about it," she said worriedly. "I'm letting everybody at the ranch down. . . ."

"Baloney," he mused, smiling. "I've got Ben and the others organized. We're making progress on your breeding program." He made a face. "John went over there today to oversee things while I was here with you."

"John's your best friend," she reminded him.

He didn't want to tell her that he was jealous of his friend. He'd wanted to thump John when he walked in and found him holding Maddie's hand. But he was trying to be reasonable. He couldn't be here and at the ranch. And John was talented with breeding livestock. He'd learned from Cole Everett, whose skills were at least equal with King Brannt's and, some people said, just a tad more scientific.

"That's nice of John," she remarked.

He forced a smile. "Yeah. He's a good guy."

She searched his eyes.

"Oh, hell," he muttered, "he's got an honors degree in animal husbandry. I've got an associate's."

She brightened. "Doesn't experience count for something?" she teased lightly.

He chuckled deep in his throat. "Nice of you, to make me feel better, when I've landed you in that hospital bed," he added with guilt in his eyes.

She squeezed his hand. "My dad used to say," she said softly, "that God sends people into our lives at various times, sometimes to help, sometimes as instruments to test us. He said that you should never blame people who cause things to happen to you, because that might be a test to teach you something you needed to know." She glanced at Odalie. "I can't be the only person who's noticed how much she's changed," she added in a low tone. "She's been my rock through all this. You have, too, but . . ."

"I understand." He squeezed her hand back, turning it over to look at the neat, clean fingernails tipping her small, capable fingers. "I've been very proud of her."

"Me, too," Maddie confessed. "Honestly this whole experience has changed the way I look at the world, at people."

"Your dad," he replied, "was a very smart man. And not just with cattle."

She smiled. "I always thought so. I do miss him."

He nodded. "I know you do."

He put her hand back on the bed. "You try to go back to sleep. Want me to call the nurse and see if she can give you something else for pain?"

She laughed softly and indicated the patch on her arm. "It's automatic. Isn't science incredible?"

"Gets more incredible every day," he agreed. He got up. "I'm going for more coffee. I won't be long."

"Thanks. For all you're doing," she said seriously.

He stared down at her with quiet, guilty eyes. "It will never be enough to make up for what happened."

"That's not true," she began.

"I'll be back in a bit." He left her brooding.

"You have to try to make Cort stop blaming himself," Maddie told Odalie the next day after she'd had breakfast and Cort had gone to the ranch for a shower and change of clothes. Odalie would go when he returned, they'd decided.

"That's going to be a tall order," the other woman said with a gentle smile.

"If there was a fault, it was Pumpkin's and mine," Maddie said doggedly. "He ran out into the road and I chased after him without paying any attention to traffic."

Odalie sat down in the seat beside the bed, her face covered in guilt. "I have a confession," she said heavily. "You're going to hate me when you hear it."

"I couldn't hate you after all you've done," came the soft reply. "It isn't possible."

Odalie flushed. "Thanks," she said in a subdued tone. She drew in a deep breath. "I drove by your place deliberately. Cort had been talking about you when I got home. I was jealous. I wanted you to see me with him." She averted her eyes. "I swear to God, if I'd had any idea what misery and grief I was going to cause, I'd never have gotten in the car at all!"

"Oh, goodness," Maddie said unsteadily. But she was much more unsettled by Odalie's jealousy than she was of her actions. It meant that Odalie cared for Cort. And everybody knew how he felt about her; he'd never made any secret of it.

But Maddie had been hurt, and Cort felt responsible. So he was paying attention to Maddie instead of Odalie out of guilt.

Everything became clear. Maddie felt her heart break. But it wasn't Odalie's fault. She couldn't force Cort not to care about her.

Odalie's clear blue eyes lifted and looked into Maddie's gray ones. "You care for him, don't you?" she asked heavily. "I'm so sorry!"

Maddie reached out a hand and touched hers. "One thing I've learned in my life is that you can't make people love you," she said softly. She drew in a long breath and stared at the ceiling. "Life just doesn't work that way."

"So it seems . . ." Odalie said, and her voice trailed away. "But you see the accident really was my fault."

Maddie shook her head. She wasn't vindictive. She smiled. "It was Pumpkin's."

Odalie felt tears streaming down her cheeks. "All this time, all I could think about is the things I did to you when we were in school. I'm so ashamed, Maddie."

Maddie was stunned.

"I put on a great act for the adults. I was shy and sweet and everybody's idea of the perfect child. But when they weren't looking, I was horrible. My parents didn't know how horrible until your father came to the house with an attorney, and laid it out for them." She grimaced. "I didn't know what happened to you. There was gossip, but it was hushed up. And gossip is usually exaggerated, you know." She picked at her fingernail, her head lowered. "I pretended that I didn't care. But I did." She looked up. "It wasn't until the accident that I really faced up to the person I'd become." She shook her own head. "I didn't like what I saw."

Maddie didn't speak. She just listened.

Odalie smiled sadly. "You know, I've spent my life listening to people rave about how pretty I was, how talented I was. But until now, nobody ever liked me because I was kind to someone."

She flushed red. "You needed me. That's new, having somebody need me." She grinned. "I really like it."

Maddie burst out laughing.

Odalie laughed, too, wiping at tears. "Anyway, I apologize wholeheartedly for all the misery I've caused you, and I'm going to work really hard at being the person I hope I can be."

"I don't know what I would have done without you," Maddie said with genuine feeling. "Nobody could have been kinder."

"Some of that was guilt. But I really like you," she said, and laughed again sheepishly. "I never knew what beautiful little creatures you could create from clay and paint."

"My hobby." She laughed.

"It's going to be a life-changing hobby. You wait."

Maddie only smiled. She didn't really believe that. But she wanted to.

Cort came back later and Odalie went home to freshen up.

Cort dropped into the chair beside Maddie's bed with a sigh. "I saw your doctor outside, doing rounds. He thinks you're progressing nicely."

She smiled. "Yes, he told me so. He said I might be able to go home in a few days. I'll still have to have physical therapy, though."

"Odalie and I will take turns bringing you here

for it," he said, answering one of her fears that her car wouldn't stand up to the demands of daily trips, much less her gas budget.

"But, Cort," she protested automatically.

He held up a hand. "It won't do any good," he assured her.

She sighed. "Okay. Thanks, then." She studied his worn face. "Odalie's been amazing, hasn't she?"

He laughed. "Oh, I could think of better words. She really shocked me. I wouldn't have believed her capable of it."

"I know."

"I'm very proud of her," he said, smiling wistfully. He was thinking what a blessing it was that Odalie hadn't shown that side of herself to him when he thought he was in love with her. Because with hindsight, he realized that it was only an infatuation. He'd had a crush on Odalie that he'd mistaken for true love.

Maddie couldn't hear his thoughts. She saw that wistful smile and thought he was seeing Odalie as he'd always hoped she could be, and that he was more in love with her than ever before.

"So am I," she replied.

He noted the odd look in her eyes and started to question it when his mother came in with Heather Everett. Both women had been visiting every day. This time they had something with them. It was a beautiful arrangement of orchids.

"We worked on it together," Heather said, smiling. She was Odalie, aged, still beautiful with blue eyes and platinum blond hair. A knockout, like dark-eyed, dark-haired Shelby Brannt, even with a sprinkle of gray hairs.

"Yes, and we're not florists, but we wanted to do something personal," Shelby added.

Heather put it on the far table, by the window, where it caught the light and looked exotic and lush.

"It's so beautiful! Thank you both," Maddie enthused.

"How are you feeling, sweetheart?" Shelby asked, hovering.

"The pain is easing, and I have feeling in my legs," she said, the excitement in her gray eyes. "The doctor thinks I'll walk again."

"That's wonderful news," Shelby said heavily. "We've been so worried."

"All of us," Heather agreed. She smiled. "It's worse for us, because Odalie was driving."

"Odalie has been my rock in a storm," Maddie said gently. "She hasn't left me, except to freshen up, since they brought me in here. I honestly don't know how I would have made it without her. Or without Cort," she added, smiling at him. "They've stopped me from brooding, cheered me up, cheered me on . . . they've been wonderful."

Shelby hugged her tall son. "Well, of course, I

think so." She laughed. "Still, it's been hard on all three families," she added quietly. "It could have been even more of a tragedy if—"

"I'm going to be fine," Maddie interrupted her.

"Yes, she is," Cort agreed. He smiled at Maddie. His dark eyes were like velvet. There was an expression in them that she'd never noticed before. Affection. Real affection.

She smiled back, shyly, and averted her eyes.

"Odalie wants you to talk to one of our friends, who has an art gallery in Dallas," Heather said. "She thinks your talent is quite incredible."

"It's not, but she's nice to say so . . ." Maddie began.

"They're her kids," Cort explained to the women, and Maddie's eyes widened. "Don't deny it, you told me so," he added, making a face at her. "She puts so much of herself into them that she can't bear to think of selling one."

"Well, I know it sounds odd, but it's like that with me and the songs I compose," Heather confessed, and flushed a little when they stared at her. "I really do put my whole heart into them. And I hesitate to share that with other people."

"Desperado owes you a lot for those wonderful songs." Shelby chuckled. "And not just money. They've made an international reputation with them."

"Thanks," Heather said. "I don't know where they come from. It's a gift. Truly a gift."

"Like Odalie's voice," Maddie replied. "She really does sing like an angel."

Heather smiled. "Thank you. I've always thought so. I wanted her to realize her dream, to sing at the Met, at the Italian opera houses." She looked introspective. "But it doesn't look like she's going to do that at all."

"Why not?" Shelby asked, curious.

Heather smiled. "I think she's hungry for a home of her own and a family. She's been talking about children lately."

"Has she?" Cort asked, amused.

He didn't seem to realize that Maddie immediately connected Heather's statement with Odalie's changed nature and Cort's pride in her. She added those facts together and came up with Cort and Odalie getting married.

It was so depressing that she had to force herself to smile and pretend that she didn't care.

"Can you imagine what beautiful children she'll have?" Maddie asked with a wistful smile.

"Well, yours aren't going to be ugly," Cort retorted. Then he remembered that he'd called Maddie that, during one of their arguments, and his face paled with shame.

Maddie averted her eyes and tried not to show what she was feeling. "Not like Odalie's," she said. "Is she thinking about getting married?" she asked Heather.

"She says she is," she replied. "I don't know if

178

she's really given it enough thought, though," she added with sadness in her tone. "Very often, we mistake infatuation for the real thing."

"You didn't," Shelby teased before anyone could react to Heather's statement. "You knew you wanted to marry Cole before you were even an adult."

Heather saw Maddie's curious glance. "Cole's mother married my father," she explained. "There was some terrible gossip spread, to the effect that we were related by blood. It broke my heart. I gave up on life. And then the truth came out, and I realized that Cole didn't hate me at all. He'd only been shoving me out of his life because he thought I was totally off-limits, and his pride wouldn't let him admit how thoroughly he'd accepted the gossip for truth."

"You made a good match." Shelby smiled.

"So did you, my friend." Heather laughed. "Your road to the altar was even more precarious than mine."

Shelby beamed. "Yes, but it was worth every tear." She hugged her son. "Look at my consolation prize!"

But when the women left, and Cort walked them out to the parking lot, Maddie was left with her fears and insecurities.

Odalie wanted to marry and raise a family. She'd seen how mature and caring Cort was, and she wanted to drive him by Maddie's house because she was jealous of her. She'd wanted Maddie to see her with Cort.

She could have cried. Once, Odalie's feelings wouldn't have mattered. But since she'd been in the hospital, Maddie had learned things about the other woman. She genuinely liked her. She was like the sister Maddie had never had.

What was she going to do? Cort seemed to like Maddie now, but she'd been hurt and it was his car that had hit her. Certainly he felt guilty. And nobody could deny how much he'd loved Odalie. He'd grieved for weeks after she left for Italy.

Surely his love for her hadn't died just because Maddie had been in an accident. He'd told Maddie that she was ugly and that she didn't appeal to him as a man, long before the wreck. That had been honest; she'd seen it in his dark eyes.

Now he was trying to make up for what had happened. He was trying to sacrifice himself to Maddie in a vain attempt to atone for her injuries. He was denying himself Odalie out of guilt.

Maddie closed her eyes. She couldn't have that. She wanted him to be happy. In fact, she wanted Odalie to be happy. Cort would be miserable if he forced himself into a relationship with Maddie that he didn't feel.

So that wasn't going to be allowed to happen. Maddie was going to make sure of it.

Chapter Nine

By the end of the second week after the accident, Maddie was back home, with a high-tech wheelchair to get around the house in.

Odalie and Cort had insisted on buying her one to use while she was recuperating, because she still couldn't walk, even though the feeling had come back into her legs. She was exhilarated with the doctor's cautious prognosis that she would probably heal completely after several months.

But she'd made her friends promise to get her an inexpensive manual wheelchair. Of course, they'd said, smiling.

Then they walked in with a salesman who asked questions, measured her and asked about her choice of colors. Oh, bright yellow, she'd teased, because she was sure they didn't make a bright yellow wheelchair. The only ones she'd seen were black and ugly and plain, and they all looked alike. She'd dreaded the thought of having to sit in one.

A few days later, the wheelchair was delivered. It came from Europe. It was the most advanced wheelchair of its type, fully motorized, able to turn in its own circumference, able to lift the user up to eye level with other people, and all-terrain. Oh, and also, bright yellow in color.

"This must have cost a fortune!" Maddie almost screamed when she saw it. "I said something inexpensive!"

Cort gave her a patient smile. "You said inexpensive. This is inexpensive," he added, glancing at Odalie.

"Cheap," the blonde girl nodded. She grinned unrepentantly. "When you get out of it, you can donate it to someone in need."

"Oh. Well." The thought that she would get out of it eventually sustained her. "I can donate it?"

Odalie nodded. She smiled.

Cort smiled, too.

"Barracudas," she concluded, looking from one to the other. "I can't get around either one of you!"

They both grinned.

She laughed. "Okay. Thanks. Really. Thanks."

"You might try it out," Odalie coaxed.

"Yes, in the direction of the hen yard," Cort added.

She looked from one of them to the other. They had very suspicious expressions. "Okay."

She was still learning to drive it, but the controls were straightforward, and it didn't take long to learn them. The salesman had come out with it, to further explain its operation.

It had big tires, and it went down steps. That was a revelation. It didn't even bump very much.

She followed Cort and Odalie over the sandy yard to the huge enclosure where her hens lived. It was grassy, despite the tendency of chickens to scratch and eat the grass, with trees on one side. The other contained multiple feeders and hanging waterers. The enormous henhouse had individual nests and cowboys cleaned it out daily. There was almost no odor, and the hens were clean and beautiful.

"My girls look very happy," Maddie said, laughing.

"They have a good reason to be happy." Cort went into the enclosure, and a minute later, he came back out, carrying a large red rooster with a big comb and immaculate feathers.

He brought him to Maddie. The rooster looked sort of like Pumpkin, but he was much bigger. He didn't seem at all bothered to be carried under someone's arm. He handed the rooster to Maddie.

She perched him on her jean-clad lap and stared at him. He cocked his head and looked at her and made a sort of purring sound.

She was aghast. She looked up at Cort wide-eyed.

"His name's Percival," Cort told her with a chuckle. "He has impeccable bloodlines."

She looked at the feathery pet again. "I've never seen a rooster this tame," she remarked.

"That's from those impeccable bloodlines." Odalie giggled. "All their roosters are like this.

They're even guaranteed to be tame, or your money back. So he's sort of returnable. But you won't need to return him. He's been here for a week and he hasn't attacked anybody yet. Considering his age, he's not likely to do it."

"His age?" Maddie prompted.

"He's two," Cort said. "Never attacked anybody on the farm for all that time. The owners' kids carry the roosters around with them all the time. They're gentled. But they're also bred for temperament. They have exceptions from time to time. But Percy's no exception. He's just sweet."

"Yes, he is." She hugged the big rooster, careful not to hug him too closely, because chickens have no diaphragm and they can be smothered if their chests are compressed for too long. "Percy, you're gorgeous!"

He made that purring sound again. Almost as if he were laughing. She handed him back to Cort. "You've got him separate from the girls?"

He nodded. "If you want biddies, we can put him with them in time for spring chicks. But they know he's nearby, and so will predators. He likes people. He hates predators. The owner says there's a fox who'll never trouble a henhouse again after the drubbing Percy gave him."

Maddie laughed with pure joy. "It will be such a relief not to have to carry a limb with me to gather eggs," she said. The smile faded. "I'll always miss Pumpkin," she said softly, "but even

I knew that something had to give eventually. He was dangerous. I just didn't have the heart to do anything about him."

"Providence did that for you," Cort replied. He smiled warmly. Maddie smiled back but she avoided his eyes.

That bothered him. He put Percy back in the enclosure in his own fenced area, very thoughtful. Maddie was polite, but she'd been backing away from him for days now. He felt insecure. He wanted to ask her what was wrong. Probably, he was going to have to do that pretty soon.

Maddie went to work on her sculptures with a vengeance, now that she had enough materials to produce anything she liked.

Her first work, though, was a tribute to her new friend. She made a fairy who looked just like Odalie, perched on a lily pad, holding a firefly. She kept it hidden when Cort and Odalie came to see her, which was pretty much every single day. It was her secret project.

She was so thrilled with it that at first she didn't even want to share it with them. Of all the pieces she'd done, this was her best effort. It had been costly, too. Sitting in one position for a long time, even in her cushy imported wheelchair, was uncomfortable and took a toll on her back.

"You mustn't stress your back muscles like this," the therapist fussed when she went in for therapy, which she did every other day. "It's too much strain so early in your recovery."

She smiled while the woman used a heat lamp and massage on her taut back. "I know. I like to sculpt things. I got overenthusiastic."

"Take frequent breaks," the therapist advised.

"I'll do that. I promise."

She was walking now, just a little at a time, but steadily. Cort had bought a unit for her bathtub that created a Jacuzzi-like effect in the water. It felt wonderful on her sore and bruised back. He'd had a bar installed, too, so that she could ease herself up out of the water and not have to worry about slipping.

Odalie brought her exotic cheeses and crackers to eat them with, having found out that cheese was pretty much Maddie's favorite food. She brought more art books, and classical music that Maddie loved.

Cort brought his guitar and sang to her. That was the hardest thing to bear. Because Maddie knew he was only doing it because he thought Maddie had feelings for him. It was humiliating that she couldn't hide them, especially since she knew that he loved Odalie and always would.

But she couldn't help but be entranced by it. She loved his deep, rich voice, loved the sound of the guitar, with its mix of nylon and steel strings. It was a classical guitar. He'd ordered it from Spain. He played as wonderfully as he sang.

When he'd played "*Recuerdos de la Alhambra*" for her, one of the most beautiful classical guitar compositions ever conceived, she wept like a baby.

"It is beautiful, isn't it?" he asked, drying her tears with a handkerchief. "It was composed by a Spaniard, Francisco Tárrega, in 1896." He smiled. "It's my favorite piece."

"Mine, too," she said. "I had a recording of guitar solos on my iPod with it. But you play it just as beautifully as that performer did. Even better than he did."

"Thanks." He put the guitar back into its case, very carefully. "From the time I was ten, there was never any other instrument I wanted to play. I worried my folks to death until they bought me one. And Morie used to go sit outside while I practiced, with earplugs in." He chuckled, referring to his sister.

"Poor Morie," she teased.

"She loves to hear me play, now. She said it was worth the pain while I learned."

She grinned. "You know, you could sing professionally."

He waved that thought away. "I'm a cattleman," he replied. "Never wanted to be anything else. The guitar is a nice hobby. But I don't think I'd enjoy playing and singing as much if I had to do it all the time."

"Good point."

"How's that sculpture coming along?"

Her eyes twinkled. "Come see."

She turned on the wheelchair and motored herself into the makeshift studio they'd furnished for her in her father's old bedroom. It had just the right airy, lighted accommodation that made it a great place to work. Besides that, she could almost feel her father's presence when she was in it.

"Don't tell her," she cautioned as she uncovered a mound on her worktable. "It's going to be a surprise."

"I promise."

She pulled off the handkerchief she'd used to conceal the little fairy sculpture. The paint was dry and the glossy finish she'd used over it gave the beautiful creature an ethereal glow.

"It looks just like her!" Cort exclaimed as he gently picked it up.

She grinned. "Do you think so? I did, but I'm too close to my work to be objective about it."

"It's the most beautiful thing you've done yet, and that's saying something." He looked down at her with an odd expression. "You really have the talent."

She flushed. "Thanks, Cort."

He put the sculpture down and bent, brushing his mouth tenderly over hers. "I have to be so careful with you," he whispered at her lips. "It's frustrating, in more ways than one."

She caught her breath. She couldn't resist him. But it was tearing her apart, to think that he might be caught in a web of deception laced by guilt. She looked up into his eyes with real pain.

He traced her lips with his forefinger. "When you're back on your feet," he whispered, "we have to talk."

She managed a smile. "Okay." Because she knew that, by then, she'd find a way to ease his guilt, and Odalie's, and step out of the picture. She wasn't going to let them sacrifice their happiness for her. That was far too much.

He kissed her again and stood up, smiling. "So when are you going to give it to her?"

"Tomorrow," she decided.

"I'll make sure she comes over."

"Thanks."

He shrugged and then smiled. "She's going to be over the moon when she sees it."

That was an understatement. Odalie cried. She turned the little fairy around and around in her elegant hands, gasping at the level of detail in the features that were so exactly like her own.

"It's the most beautiful gift I've ever been given."

She put it down, very gently, and hugged Maddie as carefully as she could. "You sweetie!" she exclaimed. "I'll never be able to thank you. It looks just like me!"

Maddie chuckled. "I'm glad you like it."

"You have to let me talk to my friend at the art gallery," Odalie said.

Maddie hesitated. "Maybe someday," she faltered. "Maybe."

"But you have so much talent, Maddie. It's such a gift."

Maddie flushed. "Thanks."

Odalie kept trying, but she couldn't move the other girl. Not at all.

"Okay," she relented. "You know your own mind. Oh, goodness, what is that?" she exclaimed, indicating a cameo lying beside another fairy, a black-haired one sitting on a riverbank holding a book.

Maddie told her the story of the antique dealer and the cameo that had no family to inherit.

"What an incredible story," Odalie said, impressed. "She's quite beautiful. You can do that, from a picture?"

Maddie laughed. "I did yours from the one in our school yearbook," she said, and this time she didn't flinch remembering the past.

Odalie looked uncomfortable, but she didn't refer to it. Perhaps in time she and Maddie could both let go of that terrible memory. "Maddie, could you do one of my great-grandmother if I brought you a picture of her? It's a commission, now . . ."

Maddie held up a hand. "No. I'd love to do it.

It's just a hobby, you know, not a job. Just bring me a picture."

Odalie's eyes were unusually bright. "Okay. I'll bring it tomorrow!"

Maddie laughed at her enthusiasm. "I'll get started as soon as I have it."

The picture was surprising. "This is your grandmother?" Maddie asked, because it didn't look anything like Odalie. The subject of the painting had red hair and pale green eyes.

"My great-grandmother," Odalie assured her, but she averted her eyes to another sculpture while she said it.

"Oh. That explains it. Yes, I can do it."

"That's so sweet of you, Maddie."

"It's nothing at all."

It took two weeks. Maddie still had periods of discomfort that kept her in bed, but she made sure she walked and moved around, as the therapist and her doctor had told her to do. It was amazing that, considering the impact of the car, she hadn't suffered a permanent disability. The swelling and inflammation had been pretty bad, as was the bruising, but she wasn't going to lose the use of her legs. The doctor was still being cautious about that prognosis. But Maddie could tell from the way she was healing that she was going to be all right. She'd never been more certain of anything.

She finished the little fairy sculpture on a Friday. She was very pleased with the result. It looked just like the photograph, but with exquisite detail. This fairy was sitting on a tree stump, with a small green frog perched on her palm. She was laughing. Maddie loved the way it had turned out. But now it was going to be hard to part with it. She did put part of herself into her sculptures. It was like giving herself away with the art.

She'd promised Odalie, though, so she had to come to terms with it.

Odalie was overwhelmed with the result. She stared at it and just shook her head. "I can't believe how skilled you are," she said, smiling at Maddie. "This is so beautiful. She'll, I mean my mother, will love it!"

"Oh, it's her grandmother," Maddie recalled.

"Yes." Odalie still wouldn't meet her eyes, but she laughed. "What a treat this is going to be! Can I take it with me?" she asked.

Maddie only hesitated for a second. She smiled. "Of course you can."

"Wonderful!"

She bent and hugged Maddie gently. "Still doing okay?" she asked worriedly.

Maddie nodded. "Getting better all the time, thanks to a small pharmacy of meds on my bedside table," she quipped.

"I'm so glad. I mean that," she said solemnly.

"The day you can walk to your car and drive it, I'll dance in the yard."

Maddie laughed. "Okay. I'll hold you to that!"

Odalie just grinned.

Cort came over every day. Saturday morning he went to the barn to study the charts he and John Everett had made. John had just come over to bring Maddie flowers. She was sitting on the porch with Great-Aunt Sadie. As soon as John arrived, Cort came back from the barn and joined the group on the porch. The way Cort glared at him was surprising.

"They'll give her allergies," Cort muttered.

John gave him a stunned look, and waved around the yard at the blooming crepe myrtle and jasmine and sunflowers and sultanas and zinnias. "Are you nuts?" he asked, wide-eyed. "Look around you! Who do you think planted all these?"

Cort's dark eyes narrowed. He jammed his hands into his jean pockets. "Well, they're not in the house, are they?" he persisted.

John just laughed. He handed the pot of flowers to Great-Aunt Sadie, who was trying not to laugh. "Can you put those inside?" he asked her with a smile. "I want to check the board in the barn and see how the breeding program needs to go."

"I sure can," Sadie replied, and she went into the house.

Maddie was still staring at John with mixed

feelings. "Uh, thanks for the flowers," she said haltingly. Cort was looking irritated.

"You're very welcome," John said. He studied her for a long moment. "You look better."

"I feel a lot better," she said. "In fact, I think I might try to walk to the barn."

"In your dreams, honey," Cort said softly. He picked her up, tenderly, and cradled her against his chest. "But I'll walk you there."

John stared at him intently. "Should you be picking her up like that?" he asked.

Cort wasn't listening. His dark eyes were probing Maddie's gray ones with deep tenderness. Neither of them was looking at John, who suddenly seemed to understand what was going on around him.

"Darn, I left my notes in the car," he said, hiding a smile. "I'll be right back."

He strode off. Cort bent his head. "I thought he'd never leave," he whispered, and brought his mouth down, hard, on Maddie's.

"Cort . . ."

"Shh," he whispered against her lips. "Don't fuss. Open your mouth . . . !"

The kiss grew hotter by the second. Maddie was clinging to his neck for dear life while he crushed her breasts into the softness of his blue-checked shirt and devoured her soft lips.

He groaned harshly, but suddenly he remembered where they were. He lifted his head, grateful that his back was to the house, and John's car. He drew in a long breath.

"I wish you weren't so fragile," he whispered. He kissed her shocked eyes shut. "I'm starving."

Her fingers teased the hair at the back of his head. "I could feed you a biscuit," she whispered.

He smiled. "I don't want biscuits." He looked at her mouth. "I want you."

Her face flamed with a combination of embarrassment and sheer delight.

"But we can talk about that later, after I've disposed of John's body," he added, turning to watch the other man approach, his eyes buried in a black notebook.

"Wh-h-hat?" she stammered, and burst out laughing at his expression.

He sighed. "I suppose no war is ever won without a few uncomfortable battles," he said under his breath.

"I found them," John said with a grin, waving the notebook. "Let's have a look at the breeding strategy you've mapped out, then."

"I put it all on the board," Cort replied. He carried Maddie into the barn and set her on her feet very carefully, so as not to jar her spine. "It's right there," he told John, nodding toward the large board where he'd indicated which bulls were to be bred to which heifers and cows.

John studied it for a long moment. He turned and looked at Cort curiously. "This is remarkable," he said. "I would have gone a different way, but yours is better."

Cort seemed surprised. "You've got a four-year degree in animal husbandry," he said. "Mine is only an associate's degree."

"Yes, but you've got a lifetime of watching your father do this." He indicated the board. "I've been busy studying and traveling. I haven't really spent that much time observing. It's rather like an internship, and I don't have the experience, even if I have the education."

"Thanks," Cort said. He was touchy about his two-year degree. He smiled. "Took courses in diplomacy, too, did you?" he teased.

John bumped shoulders with him. "You're my best friend," he murmured. "I'd never be the one to try to put you down."

Cort punched his shoulder gently. "Same here."

Maddie had both hands on her slender hips as she stared at the breeding chart. "Would either of you like to try to translate this for me?" She waved one hand at the blackboard. "Because it looks like Martian to me!"

Both men burst out laughing.

Cort had to go out of town. He was worried when he called Maddie to tell her, apologizing for his absence.

"Mom and Dad will look out for you while I'm gone," he promised. "If you need anything, you call them. I'll phone you when I get to Denver."

Her heart raced. "Okay."

"Will you miss me?" he teased.

She drew in a breath. "Of course," she said.

There was a pause. "I'll miss you more," he said quietly. His deep voice was like velvet. "What do you want me to bring you from Denver?"

"Yourself."

There was a soft chuckle. "That's a deal. Talk to you later."

"Have a safe trip."

He sighed. "At least Dad isn't flying me. He flies like he drives. But we'll get there."

The plural went right over her head. She laughed. She'd heard stories about King Brannt's driving. "It's safer than driving, everybody says so."

"In my dad's case, it's actually true. He flies a lot better than he drives."

"I heard that!" came a deep voice from beside him.

"Sorry, Dad," Cort replied. "See you, Maddie."

He hung up. She held the cell phone to her ear for an extra minute, just drinking in the sound of his voice promising to miss her.

While Cort was away, Odalie didn't come, either. But even though she called, Maddie missed her daily visits. She apologized over the phone. She was actually out of town, but her mother had volunteered to do any running-around that Maddie needed if Sadie couldn't go.

Maddie thanked her warmly. But when she hung up she couldn't help but wonder at the fact that Cort and Odalie were out of town at the same time. Had Odalie gone to Denver with Cort and they didn't want to tell her? It was worrying.

She rode her wheelchair out to the hen enclosure. Ben was just coming out of it with the first of many egg baskets. There were a lot of hens, and her customer list for her fresh eggs was growing by the week.

"That's a lot of eggs," she ventured.

He chuckled. "Ya, and I still have to wash 'em and check 'em for cracks."

"I like Percy," she remarked.

"I love Percy," Ben replied. "Never saw such a gentle rooster."

"Thanks. For what you did for Pumpkin's grave," she said, averting her eyes. She still cried easily when she talked about him.

"It was no problem at all, Miss Maddie," he said gently.

She looked over her hens with proud eyes. "My girls look good."

"They do, don't they?" he agreed, then added, "Well, I should get to work."

"Ben, do you know where Odalie went?" she asked suddenly.

He bit his lip.

"Come on," she prodded. "Tell me."

He looked sad. "She went to Denver, Miss Maddie. Heard it from her dad when I went to pick up feed in town."

Maddie's heart fell to her feet. But she smiled. "She and Cort make a beautiful couple," she remarked, and tried to hide the fact that she was dying inside.

"Guess they do," he said. He tried to say something else, but he couldn't get the words to come out right. "I'll just go get these eggs cleaned."

She nodded. The eyes he couldn't see were wet with tears.

It seemed that disaster followed disaster. While Cort and Odalie were away, bills flooded the mailbox. Maddie almost passed out when she saw the hospital bill. Even the minimum payment was more than she had in the bank.

"What are we going to do?" she wailed.

Sadie winced at her expression. "Well, we'll just manage," she said firmly. "There's got to be something we can sell that will help pay those bills." She didn't add that Cort and Odalie had promised they were taking care of all that. But they were out of town, and Sadie knew that Maddie's pride would stand in the way of asking them for money. She'd never do it.

"There is something," Maddie said heavily. She looked up at Sadie.

"No," Sadie said shortly. "No, you can't!"

"Look at these bills, Sadie," she replied, and spread them out on the table. "There's nothing I can hock, nothing I can do that will make enough money fast enough to cover all this. There just isn't anything else to do."

"You aren't going to talk to that developer fellow?"

"Heavens, no!" Maddie assured her. "I'll call a real estate agent in town."

"I think that's . . ."

Just as she spoke, a car pulled up in the yard.

"Well, speak of the devil," Maddie muttered.

The developer climbed out of his car, looked around and started for the front porch.

"Do you suppose we could lock the door and pretend to be gone?" Sadie wondered aloud.

"No. We're not hiding. Let him in," Maddie said firmly.

"Don't you give in to his fancy talk," Sadie advised.

"Never in a million years. Let him in."

The developer, Arthur Lawson, came in the door with a smug look on his face. "Miss Lane," he greeted. He smiled like a crocodile. "Bad news does travel fast. I heard you were in an accident and that your bills are piling up. I believe I can help you."

Maddie looked at Sadie. Her expression was eloquent.

Archie Lawson grinned like the barracuda he was.

"I heard that your neighbors have gone away together," he said with mock sympathy. "Just left you with all those medical bills to pay, did they?"

Maddie felt terrible. She didn't want to say anything unkind about Odalie and Cort. They'd done more than most people could have expected of them. But Maddie was left with the bills, and she had no money to pay them with. She'd read about people who didn't pay their hospital bill on time and had to deal with collectors' agencies. She was terrified.

"They don't say I have to pay them at once," Maddie began.

"Yes, but the longer you wait, the higher the interest they charge," he pointed out.

"Interest?"

"It's such and such a percent," he continued. He sat down without being asked in her father's old easy chair. "Let me spell it out for you. I can write you a check that will cover all those medical bills, the hospital bill, everything. All you have to do is sign over the property to me. I'll even take care of the livestock. I'll make sure they're sold to people who will take good care of them."

"I don't know," Maddie faltered. She was torn. It was so quick . . .

"Maddie, can I talk to you for a minute?"

Sadie asked tersely. "It's about supper," she lied.

"Okay."

She excused herself and followed Sadie into the kitchen.

Sadie closed the door. "Listen to me, don't you do that until you talk to Mr. Brannt," Sadie said firmly. "Don't you dare!"

"But, Sadie," she said in anguish, "we can't pay the bills, and we can't expect the Brannts and the Everetts to keep paying them forever!"

"Cort said he'd take care of the hospital bill, at least," Sadie reminded her.

"Miss Lane?" Lawson called. "I have to leave soon!"

"Don't let him push you into this," Sadie cautioned. "Make him wait. Tell him you have to make sure the estate's not entailed before you can sell, you'll have to talk to your lawyer!"

Maddie bit her lower lip.

"Tell him!" Sadie said, gesturing her toward the porch.

Maddie took a deep breath and Sadie opened the door for her to motor through.

"Sadie was reminding me that we had a couple of outstanding liens on the property after Dad died," Maddie lied. "I'll have to talk to our attorney and make sure they've been lifted before I can legally sell it to you."

"Oh." He stood up. "Well." He glared. "You didn't mention that earlier."

"I didn't think you thought I was going to sell the ranch today," Maddie said, and with a bland smile. "That's all. You wouldn't want to find out later that you didn't actually own it . . . ?"

"No. Of course not." He made a face. "All right, I'll be back in, say, two days? Will that give you enough time?"

"Yes," Maddie said.

He picked up his briefcase and looked around the living room. "This house will have to be torn down. But if you want some pictures and stuff, I can let you have it after we wrap up the sale. The furniture's no loss." He laughed coldly. "I'll be in touch. And if your answer is no—well, don't be surprised if your cattle suddenly come down with unusual diseases. Anthrax always comes to mind . . . And if federal agencies have to be called in, your operation will be closed down immediately."

He left and Maddie had to bite back curses. "The furniture's no loss," she muttered. "These are antiques! And anthrax! What kind of horrible person would infect defenseless animals!" Maddie went inside, a chill settling in her heart.

"Nasty man. You can't let him have our house!" Sadie glared out the window as the developer drove off.

Maddie leaned back in her chair. "I wish I didn't," she said heavily. "But I don't know what else to do." She felt sick to her soul at the man's threats. "Cort is going to marry Odalie, you know."

Sadie wanted to argue, but she didn't know how to. It seemed pretty obvious that if he hadn't told Maddie he was leaving with Odalie, he had a guilty conscience and was trying to shield her from the truth.

"Should have just told you, instead of sneaking off together," Sadie muttered.

"They didn't want to hurt me," Maddie said heavily. "It's pretty obvious how I feel about Cort, you know."

"Still . . ."

Maddie looked at the bills lying open on the table. She leaned forward with her face in her hands. Her heart was breaking. At least she might be able to walk eventually. But that still left the problem of how she was going to walk herself out of this financial mess. The ranch was all she had left for collateral.

Collateral! She turned to Sadie. "We can take out a mortgage, can't we?" she asked Sadie.

Sadie frowned. "I don't know. Best you should call the lawyer and find out."

"I'll do that right now!"

She did at least have hope that there were options. A few options, at least.

But the lie she'd told Lawson turned out to be the truth.

"I'm really sorry, Maddie," Burt Davies told her. "But your dad did take out a lien on the property when he bought that last seed bull. I've been keeping up the payments out of the ranch revenues when I did the bills for you the past few months."

"You mean, I can't sell or even borrow on the ranch."

"You could sell," he admitted. "If you got enough for it that would pay off the lien . . . But, Maddie, that land's been in your family for generations. You can't mean to sell it."

She swallowed. "Burt, I've got medical bills I can't begin to pay."

"Odalie and Cort are taking care of those," he reminded her. "Legally, even if not morally, they're obligated to."

"Yes, but, they're getting married, don't you see?" she burst out. "I can't tie them up with my bills."

"You can and you will, if I have to go to court for you," Burt said firmly. "The accident wasn't your fault."

"Yes, it was," she said in a wan tone. "I ran out in the road to save my stupid rooster, who died anyway. As for guilt, Odalie and Cort have done everything humanly possible for me since the wreck. Nobody could fault them for that."

"I know, but . . ."

"If I sell the ranch," she argued gently, "I can

pay off all my debts and I won't owe anyone anything."

"That's bad legal advice. You should never try to act as your own attorney."

She laughed. "Yes, I know. Okay, I'll think about it for a couple of days," she said.

"You think about it hard," he replied. "No sense in letting yourself be forced into a decision you don't want to make."

"All right. Thanks, Burt."

She hung up. "Life," she told the room at large, "is just not fair."

The next day, Ben came walking in with a sad expression. "Got bad news," he said.

"What now?" Maddie asked with a faint smile.

"Lost two more purebred cows. They wandered off."

"All right, that's more than coincidence," she muttered. She moved to the phone, picked it up and called King Brannt.

"How many cows does that make?" King asked, aghast.

"Four, in the past few weeks," she said. "Something's not right."

"I agree. I'll get our computer expert to check those recordings and see if he can find anything."

"Thanks, Mr. Brannt."

He hesitated. "How are things over there?"

She hesitated, too. "Just fine," she lied. "Fine."

"Cort's coming home day after tomorrow," he added.

"I hope he and Odalie have had a good time," she said, and tried not to sound as hurt as she felt. "They've both been very kind to me. I owe them a lot."

"Maddie," he began slowly, "about that trip they took—"

"They're my friends," she interrupted. "I want them to be happy. Look I have to go, okay? But if you find out anything about my cows, can you call me?"

"Sure."

"Thanks, Mr. Brannt."

She hung up. She didn't think she'd ever felt so miserable in her whole young life. She loved Cort. But he was never going to be hers. She realized now that he'd been pretending, to keep her spirits up so that she wouldn't despair. But he'd always loved Odalie, and she'd always known it. She couldn't expect him to give up everything he loved just to placate an injured woman, out of guilt. She wasn't going to let him do it.

And Odalie might have been her enemy once, but that was certainly no longer the case. Odalie had become a friend. She couldn't have hard feelings toward her. . . .

Oh, what a bunch of bull, she told herself angrily. Of course she had hard feelings. She loved Cort. She wanted him! But he loved Odalie and that was never going to change. How would it feel, to let a man hang around just because he felt guilty that you'd been hurt? Knowing every day that he was smiling and pretending to care, when he really wanted that beautiful golden girl, Odalie Everett, and always would?

No. That would cheat all three of them. She had to let him go. He belonged to Odalie, and Maddie had always known it. She was going to sell the ranch to that terrible developer and make herself homeless out of pride, because she didn't want her friends to sacrifice any more than they already had for her.

That developer, could he have been responsible for her lost cows? But why would he hurt the livestock when he was hoping to buy the ranch? No. It made no sense. None at all.

Later, with her door closed, she cried herself to sleep. She couldn't stop thinking about Cort, about how tender he'd been to her, how kind. Surely he hadn't been able to pretend the passion she felt in his long, hard, insistent kisses? Could men pretend to want a woman?

She wished she knew. She wanted to believe that his hints at a shared future had been honest and real. But she didn't dare trust her instincts. Not when Cort had taken Odalie with him to Denver and hidden it from Maddie.

He hadn't wanted her to know. That meant he knew it would hurt her feelings and he couldn't bear to do it, not after all she'd been through.

She wiped her eyes. Crying wasn't going to solve anything. After all, what did she have to be sad about? There was a good chance that she would be able to walk normally again, when she was through recuperating. She'd still have Great-Aunt Sadie, and the developer said that he'd let her have her odds and ends out of the house.

The developer. She hated him. He was willing to set her up, to let her whole herd of cattle be destroyed, her breeding stock, just to get his hands on the ranch. She could tell someone, Mr. Brannt, maybe. But it would be her word against Lawson's. She had so much to lose. What if he could actually infect her cattle? Better to let her cattle be sold at auction to someone than risk having them destroyed. She couldn't bear to step on a spider, much less watch her prize cattle, her father's prize cattle, be exterminated.

No, she really didn't have a choice. She was going to lose the ranch one way or another, to the developer or to bill collectors.

She got up and went to the kitchen to make coffee. It was two in the morning, but it didn't matter. She was never going to sleep anyway.

She heard a sound out in the yard. She wished she kept a dog. She'd had one, but it had died not long after her father did. There was nothing to alert her to an intruder's presence anymore. She turned out the lights and motored to the window, hoping the sound of the wheelchair wouldn't be heard outside.

She saw something shadowy near the barn. That was where the surveillance equipment was set up.

She turned on all the outside lights, opened the door and yelled, "Who's out there?!" The best defense was offense, she told herself.

There was startled movement, a dark blur going out behind the barn. Without a second thought, she got her cell phone and called the sheriff.

The sheriff's department came, and so did King Brannt. He climbed out of his ranch pickup with another man about two steps behind the tall deputy.

Maddie rolled onto the porch. She'd been afraid to go outside until help arrived. She was no match, even with two good legs, for someone bent upon mischief.

"Miss Lane?" the deputy asked.

"Yes, sir," she said. "Someone was out here. I turned on the outside lights and yelled. Whoever it was ran."

The deputy's lips made a thin line.

"Yes, I know," she said heavily. "Stupid thing to do, opening the door. But I didn't go outside, and the screen was latched."

He didn't mention that any intruder could have gone through that latched screen like it was tissue paper.

"Miss Lane's had some threats," King commented. "This is Blair, my computer expert. We set up surveillance cameras on the ranch at cross fences to see if we could head off trouble." He smiled. "Looks like we might have succeeded."

"Have you noticed anything suspicious?" the deputy asked.

She grimaced. "Well, I've had a couple of cows found dead. Predators," she said, averting her eyes.

"Anyone prowling around the house, any break-ins?" he persisted.

"No, sir."

The deputy turned to King. "Mr. Brannt, I'd like to see what those cameras of yours picked up, if anything."

"Sure. Come on, Blair." He turned to Maddie. "You should go back inside, honey," he said gently. "Just in case."

"Okay." She went very quickly. She didn't want any of the men to ask her more questions. She was afraid of what Lawson might do if he was backed into a corner. She didn't want the government to come over and shut her cattle operation down, even if it meant giving away the ranch.

Later, the deputy came inside, asked more questions and had her write out a report for him in her own words. He took that, and statements from King and Blair and told Maddie to call if she heard anything else.

"Did you find anything?" she asked worriedly.

"No," the deputy said. "But my guess is that someone meant to disable that surveillance equipment."

"Mine, too," King replied. "Which is why I've just sent several of my cowboys out to ride fence lines and watch for anything suspicious."

"That's very nice of you," she commented.

He shrugged. "We're neighbors and I like your breeding bulls," he told her.

"Well, thanks, just the same."

"If you think of anything else that would help us, please get in touch with me," the deputy said, handing her a card.

"I'll do that," she promised. "And thanks again."

King didn't leave when the deputy did. Sadie was making coffee in the kitchen, her face lined with worry.

"It will be all right," she assured the older woman.

"No, it won't," Sadie muttered. She glanced at Maddie. "You should tell him the truth. He's the one person who could help you!"

"Sadie!" Maddie groaned.

King pulled Blair aside, spoke to him in whispers, and sent him off. He moved into the kitchen, straddled a chair at the table and perched his Stetson on a free chair.

"Okay," he said. "No witnesses. Let's have it."

Maddie went pale.

King laughed softly. "I'm not an ogre. If you want my word that I won't tell anyone what you say, you have it."

Maddie bit her lower lip. "That developer," she said after a minute. "He said that he could bring in a federal agency and prove that my cattle had anthrax."

"Only if he put it there to begin with," King said, his dark eyes flashing with anger.

"That's what I think he means to do," she said. "I don't know what to do. The bills are just burying me . . ."

He held up a hand. "Cort and Odalie are taking care of those," he said.

"Yes, but they've done too much already, I'm not a charity case!" she burst out.

"It was an accident that they caused, Maddie," he said gently.

"I caused it, by running into the road," she said miserably.

"Accidents are things that don't happen on purpose," he said with a faint grin. "Now, listen, whatever trouble you're in, that developer has no right to make threats to do harm to your cattle."

"It would be my word against his," she sighed.

"I'd take your word against anyone else's, in a

heartbeat," he replied. "You let me handle this. I know how to deal with people like Lawson."

"He's really vindictive."

"He won't get a chance to be vindictive. I promise." He got up. "I won't stay for coffee, Sadie, I've got a lot of phone calls to make."

"Thanks, Mr. Brannt," Maddie said gently. "Thanks a lot."

He put a hand on her shoulder. "We take care of our own," he said. "Cort will be back day after tomorrow."

"So will that developer," she said worriedly. So many complications, she was thinking. Poor Cort, he'd feel even more guilty.

"He won't stay long," King drawled, and he grinned. "Cort will make sure of that, believe me."

Chapter Ten

Maddie was on pins and needles Saturday morning. It was worrying enough to know that Cort and Odalie were coming back. She'd have to smile and pretend to be happy for them, even though her heart was breaking.

But also she was going to have to face the developer. She didn't know what King Brannt had in mind to save her from him. She might have to go through with signing the contracts to ensure that her poor cattle weren't infected. She hadn't slept a wink.

She and Sadie had coffee and then Maddie wandered around the house in her wheelchair, making ruts.

"Will you relax?" Sadie said. "I know it's going to be all right. You have to trust that Mr. Brannt knows what to do."

"I hope so. My poor cattle!"

"Is that a car?"

Even as she spoke a car drove up in front of the house and stopped. "Mr. Lawson, no doubt. I hope he's wearing body armor," she muttered, and she wheeled her chair to the front porch.

But it wasn't the developer. It was Odalie and Cort. They were grinning from ear to ear as they climbed out of his Jaguar and came to the porch.

Just what I need right now, Maddie thought miserably. But she put on a happy face. "You're both home again. And I guess you have news?" she added. "I'm so happy for you."

"For us?" Cort looked at Odalie and back at Maddie blankly. "Why?"

They followed her into the house. She turned the chair around and swallowed. "Well," she began uneasily.

Odalie knew at once what she thought. She came forward. "No, it's not like that," she said quickly. "There was a doll collectors' convention at the hotel where the cattlemen were meeting. I want you to see this." She pulled a check out of her purse and handed it to Maddie.

It was a good thing she was sitting down. The check was for five figures. Five high figures. She looked at Odalie blankly.

"The fairy," she said, smiling. "I'm sorry I wasn't honest with you. It wasn't my great-grandmother's picture. It was a collector's. He wanted a fairy who looked like her to add to his collection, and I said I knew someone who would do the perfect one. So I flew to Denver to take him the one you made from the photograph." Odalie's blue eyes were soft. "He cried. He said the old lady was the light of his life . . . She was the only person in his family who didn't laugh and disown him when he said he wanted to go into the business of doll collecting. She encouraged him to follow his dream. He's worth millions now and all because he followed his dream." She nodded at the check. "He owns a doll boutique in Los Angeles. He ships all over the world. He said he'd pay that—" she indicated the check again "—for every fairy you made for him. And he wants to discuss licensing and branding. He thinks you can make a fortune with these. He said so."

Maddie couldn't even find words. The check would pay her medical bills, buy feed and pay taxes. It would save the ranch. She was sobbing and she didn't even realize it until Odalie took the check back and motioned to Cort.

Cort lifted her out of the wheelchair and cradled her against him. "You'll blot the ink off the check with those tears, sweetheart." He chuckled, and kissed them away. "And just for the record, Odalie and I aren't getting married."

"You aren't?" she asked with wet eyes.

"We aren't." Odalie giggled. "He's my friend. I love him. But not like that," she added softly.

"And she's my friend," Cort added. He smiled down at Maddie. "I went a little goofy over her, but, then, I got over it."

"Gee, thanks," Odalie said with amused sarcasm.

"You know what I mean." He laughed. "You're beautiful and talented."

"Not as talented as *our* friend over there." She indicated Maddie, with a warm smile. "She has magic in her hands."

"And other places," Cort mused, looking pointedly at her mouth.

She hid her face against him. He cuddled her close.

"Oh, dear," Sadie said from the doorway. "Maddie, he's back! What are you going to tell him?"

"Tell who?" Cort asked. He turned. His face grew hard. "Oh. Him. My dad gave me an earful about him when I got home."

He put Maddie gently back down into the wheelchair.

"You didn't encourage him?" he asked her.

She grimaced. "The medical bills and doctor bills and feed bills all came in at once," she began miserably. "I couldn't even pay taxes. He offered me a fortune . . ."

"We're paying the medical bills," Odalie told her firmly. "We even said so."

"It's not right to ask you," Maddie said stubbornly.

"That's okay. You're not asking. We're telling," Odalie said.

"Exactly." Cort was looking more dangerous by the second as the developer got out of his car with a briefcase. "My dad said you've had more cows killed over here, too."

"Yes." She was so miserable she could hardly talk.

"Dad found out a lot more than that about him. He was arrested up in Billings, Montana, on charges of intimidation and poisoning in another land deal," Cort added. "He's out on bond, but apparently it didn't teach him a thing."

"Well, he threatened to plant anthrax in my herd and have the feds come out and destroy them," she said sadly. "He says if I don't sell to him, he'll do it. I think he will."

"He might have," Cort said mysteriously.

"Good thing my dad has a real suspicious nature and watches a lot of spy films."

"Excuse me?" Maddie inquired.

He grinned. "Wait and see, honey." He bent and kissed the tip of her nose.

Odalie laughed softly. "One fried developer, coming right up," she teased, and it was obvious that she wasn't jealous of Maddie at all.

There was a tap at the door and the developer walked right in. He was so intent on his contracts that he must not have noticed the other car in the driveway. "Miss Lane, I've brought the paper . . . work—" He stopped dead when he saw her companions.

"You can take your paperwork and shove it," Cort said pleasantly. He tilted his Stetson over one eye and put both hands on his narrow hips. "Or you can argue. Personally, I'd love it if you argued."

"She said she wanted to sell," the developer shot back. But he didn't move a step closer.

"She changed her mind," Cort replied.

"You changed it for her," the developer snarled. "Well, she can just change it right back. Things happen sometimes when people don't make the right decisions."

"You mean diseases can be planted in cattle?" Odalie asked sweetly.

The older man gave her a wary look. "What do you mean?"

"Maddie told us how you threatened her," Cort said evenly.

Lawson hesitated. "You can't prove that."

Cort smiled. "I don't have to." He pulled out a DVD in a plastic sleeve and held it up. "You're very trusting, Lawson. I mean, you knew there was surveillance equipment all over the ranch, but you didn't guess the house and porch were wired as well?"

Lawson looked a lot less confident. "You're bluffing."

Cort didn't look like he was bluffing. "My dad has a call in to the district attorney up in Billings, Montana. I believe you're facing indictment there for the destruction of a purebred herd of Herefords because of suspected anthrax?"

"They can't prove that!"

"I'm afraid they can," Cort replied. "There are two witnesses, one of whom used to work with you," he added easily. "He's willing to testify to save his butt." He held up the DVD. "This may not be admissible in court, but it will certainly help to encourage charges against you here for the loss of Miss Lane's purebred stock."

"You wouldn't dare!" the developer said harshly.

"I would dare," Cort replied.

The developer gripped his briefcase tighter. "On second thought," he said, looking around with disdain, "I've decided I don't want this property. It's not good enough for the sort of development

I have in mind, and the location is terrible for business. Sorry," he spat at Maddie. "I guess you'll have to manage some other way to pay your medical bills."

"Speaking of medical bills," Cort said angrily, and stepped forward.

"Now, Cort," Maddie exclaimed.

The developer turned and almost ran out of the house to his car. He fumbled to start it and managed to get it in gear just before Cort got to him. He sped out the driveway, fishtailing all the way.

Cort was almost bent over double laughing when he went back into the house. He stopped when three wide-eyed females gaped at him worriedly.

"Oh, I wasn't going to kill him," he said, still laughing. "But I didn't mind letting him think I might. What do you want to bet that he's out of town by tonight and can't be reached by telephone?"

"I wouldn't bet against that," Odalie agreed.

"Me, neither," Sadie said.

"Dad said that Lawson's in more trouble than he can manage up in Billings already. I don't expect he'll wait around for more charges to be filed here."

"Are you going to turn that DVD over to the district attorney?" she asked, nodding toward the jacketed disc.

He glanced at her. "And give up my best performance of '*Recuerdos de la Alhambra*'?" he exclaimed. "I'll never get this good a recording again!"

Maddie's eyes brightened. "You were bluffing!"

"For all I was worth." He chuckled.

"Cort, you're wonderful!"

He pursed his lips. "Am I, now?"

"We could take a vote," Odalie suggested. "You've got mine."

"And mine!" Sadie agreed. "Oh, Maddie, you'll have a way to make a living now," she exclaimed, indicating the little fairy. "You won't have to sell our ranch!"

"No, but we still have the problem of running it," Maddie said heavily. "If I'm going to be spending my life sculpting, and thanks to you two, I probably will—" she grinned "—who's going to manage the ranch?"

"I think we can work something out about that," Cort told her, and his dark eyes were flashing with amusement. "We'll talk about it later."

"Okay," she said. "Maybe Ben could manage it?"

Cort nodded. "He's a good man, with a good business head. We'll see."

We'll see? She stared at him as if she'd never seen him before. It was an odd statement. But before she could question it, Sadie went into the kitchen.

"Who wants chocolate pound cake?" she asked.

Three hands went up, and all discussion about the ranch went away.

Maddie wanted to know all about the doll collector. He was a man in his fifties, very distinguished and he had a collection that was famous all over the world.

"There are magazines devoted to collectors," Odalie said excitedly. "They showcased his collection last year. I met him when we were at the Met last year during opera season. We spoke and he said that he loved small, very intricate work. When I saw your sculptures, I remembered him. I looked him up on his website and phoned him. He said he was always looking for new talent, but he wanted to see what you could do. So I asked him for a photo of someone he'd like made into a sculpture and he faxed me the one I gave you."

"I will never be able to repay you for this," Maddie said fervently.

"Maddie, you already have, over and over," Odalie said softly. "Most especially with that little fairy statue that looks just like me." She shook her head. "I've never owned anything so beautiful."

"Thanks."

"Besides, you're my best friend," Odalie said with a gamine grin. "I have to take care of you."

Maddie felt all warm inside. "I'll take care

of you, if you ever need me to," she promised.

Odalie flushed. "Thanks."

"This is great cake," Cort murmured. "Can you cook?" he asked Maddie.

"Yes, but not so much right now." She indicated the wheelchair with a grimace.

"Give it time," he said gently. He smiled, and his whole face grew radiant as he looked at her. "You'll be out of that thing before you know it."

"You think so?" she asked.

He nodded. "Yes, I do."

She smiled. He smiled back. Odalie smiled into her cake and pretended not to notice that they couldn't take their eyes off each other.

Odalie said her goodbyes and gave Maddie the collector's telephone number so that she could thank him personally for giving her fairy a good home. But Cort lingered.

He bent over the wheelchair, his hands on the arms, and looked into Maddie's eyes. "Later we'll talk about going behind my back to do business with a crook."

"I was scared. And not just that he might poison my cattle. There were so many bills!"

He brushed his mouth over her lips. "I told you I'd take care of all those bills."

"But they all came due, and you've done so much . . . I couldn't ask . . ."

He was kissing her. It made talking hard.

She reached up with cold, nervous hands and framed his face in them. She looked into his eyes and saw secrets revealed there. Her breath caught. "It isn't Odalie," she stammered. "It's me."

He nodded. And he didn't smile. "It was always you. I just didn't know it until there was a good chance that I was going to lose you." He smiled tightly then. "Couldn't do that. Couldn't live, if you didn't."

She bit her lip, fighting tears.

He kissed them away. "I don't have a life without you," he whispered at her nose. "So we have to make plans."

"When?" she asked, bursting with happiness.

"When you're out of that wheelchair," he said. He gave her a wicked smile. "Because when we start talking, things are apt to get, well, physical." He wiggled his eyebrows.

She laughed.

He laughed.

He kissed her affectionately and stood back up. "I'll drive Odalie home. I'll call you later. And I'll see you tomorrow. And the day after. And the day after. And the day after that . . ."

"And the day after that?" she prompted.

"Don't get pushy," he teased.

He threw up a hand and went out to the car. This time, when he drove off with Odalie, Maddie didn't go through pangs of jealousy. The look in his eyes had been as sweet as a promise.

Epilogue

Physical therapy seemed to go on forever. The days turned to weeks, the leaves began to fall. The cows grew big with calves. Rain had come in time for some of the grain crops to come to harvest, and there would be enough hay, hopefully, to get them through the winter.

Maddie's legs were growing stronger. Little by little, she made progress.

Odalie and Cort were still around, prodding her, keeping her spirits up during the long mending process. She didn't let herself get discouraged. She created new fairies and Odalie shipped them off, carefully packed, to a man named Angus Moore, who acted as Maddie's agent and sold her dainty little creations for what amounted to a small fortune for the artist.

The developer, sure enough, left town and left no forwarding address. Gossip was that the authorities wanted to talk to him about several cases of dead cattle on properties he'd tried to buy in several states. Maddie hoped they caught up with him one day.

Meanwhile, Cort came over every night for supper. He brought his guitar most nights, and

226

serenaded Maddie on the porch until the nights got too cold for that. Then he serenaded her in the living room, by the fireplace with its leaping flames while she curled up under a blanket on the sofa.

From time to time, when Sadie was occupied in the kitchen, he curled up under the blanket with her.

She loved his big hands smoothing her bare skin under her shirt, the warmth and strength of them arousing sensations that grew sweeter by the day. He was familiar to her now. She had no fear of his temper. He didn't lose it with her, although he'd been volatile about a man who left a gate open and cattle poured through it onto the highway. At least none of the cattle was injured, and no cars were wrecked.

"He was just a kid," Cort murmured against her collarbone. "He works for us after school. Usually does a pretty good job, too, cleaning out the stables."

She arched her back and winced.

"Damn." He lifted his head and his hands stilled on her body. "Too soon."

She looked miserable.

He laughed. He peered toward the doorway before he slid the hem of her T-shirt up under her chin and looked at the pert little breasts he'd uncovered. "Buried treasure," he whispered, "and I'm a pirate . . ."

She moaned.

"Stop that. She'll hear you."

She bit her lip and gave him an anguished look. He grinned before he bent his head again, producing even more eloquent sounds that were, thankfully, soon muffled by his mouth.

But things between them were heating up more every day. She had his shirt unbuttoned just before he eased over her. Her hard-tipped breasts nestled into the thick hair on his muscular chest and one long, powerful leg eased between both of hers. He levered himself down very gently while he was kissing her, but she felt the quick, hard swell of him as he began to move helplessly on her, grinding his hips into hers.

"Oh, God," he bit off. He jerked himself back and up, to sit beside her on the sofa with his head bent, shuddering.

"I'm sorry," she whispered shakily.

He drew in short, harsh breaths while his hands worked at buttoning up the shirt. "Well, I'm not," he murmured, glancing down at her. He groaned. "Honey, you have to cover those up or we're going to be back at first base all over again!"

She looked down and flushed a little as she pulled her shirt down and fumbled behind her to do up the bra again. "First base."

He laughed softly. "First base."

She beamed at him. "I'm getting better every day. It won't be long."

"It had better not be," he sighed. "I think I'll die of it pretty soon."

"No!"

"Just kidding." He turned on the sofa and looked down at her with warm, dark, possessive eyes. "I talked to a minister."

"You did? What did he have to say?"

He traced her nose. "We have to have a marriage license first."

Her heart jumped. They'd been kissing and petting for quite a long time, and he'd insinuated, but he'd never actually asked.

"I thought we might get one with flowers and stuff. You know. So it would look nice framed on the wall."

"Framed."

He nodded. His eyes were steady on her face. "Madeline Edith Lane, will you do me the honor of becoming my wife?" he asked softly.

She fought tears. "Yes," she whispered. "Yes!"

He brushed the tears away, his eyes so dark they seemed black. "I'll love you all my life," he whispered. "I'll love you until the sun burns out."

"I'll love you longer," she whispered back, and it was all there, in her eyes and his.

He smiled slowly. "And we'll have beautiful kids," he said softly. He pushed back her hair. "Absolutely beautiful. Like you."

Now she was really bawling.

He pulled her gently into his arms and across his lap, and rocked her and kissed away the tears.

Sadie came walking in with coffee and stopped dead. "Oh, goodness, what's wrong?"

"I told her we were going to have beautiful kids," he said with a chuckle. "She's very emotional."

"Beautiful kids? You're going to get married?" Sadie exclaimed.

"Yes." Maddie smiled.

"Whoopee!"

"Oh, dear!" Maddie exclaimed.

Sadie looked down at the remains of the glass coffeepot and two ceramic mugs. "Oh, dear," she echoed.

Cort just laughed. But then, like the gentleman he was, he went to help Sadie clean up the mess.

They were married at Christmas. Maddie was able to wear an exquisite designer gown that Odalie had insisted on buying for her, as her "something new." It was an A-line gown of white satin with cap sleeves and a lacy bodice that went up to encase her throat like a high-necked Victorian dress.

There was a train, also of delicate white lace, and a fingertip veil with lace and appliquéd roses. She wore lace gloves and carried a bouquet of white roses. There was a single red rose in the center of the bouquet. One red rose for true love,

Cort had insisted, and white ones for purity because in a modern age of easy virtue, Maddie was a throwback to Victorian times. She went to her marriage a virgin, and never apologized once for not following the crowd.

She walked down the aisle on the arm of Cole Everett, who had volunteered to give her away. Odalie was her maid of honor. Heather Everett and Shelby Brannt were her matrons of honor. Four local girls she'd known all her life were bridesmaids, and John Everett was Cort's best man.

At an altar with pots of white and red roses they were married in the local Methodist church, where all three families were members. The minister had preached the funeral of most of their deceased kin. He was elderly and kind, and beloved of the community.

When he pronounced Cort and Maddie man and wife, Cort lifted the veil, ignoring the flash from the professional photographer's camera, and closed in to kiss his new bride.

Nobody heard him when he bent, very low, and whispered, "First base."

Nobody heard the soft, mischievous laughter the comment provoked from the bride. There was a huge reception. John Everett stopped by the table where Cort and Maddie were cutting the wedding cake.

"So, tell me, Cort," John said when the photographer finished shooting the cake-eating segment, "if I'm really the best man, why are you married to my girl?"

"Now, a remark like that could get you punched," Cort teased, catching the other man around the neck, "even at a wedding."

John chuckled, embracing him in a bear hug. "I was just kidding. No doubt in my mind from the beginning where her heart was." He indicated a beaming Maddie.

Cort glanced at her and smiled. "What an idiot I was," he said, shaking his head. "I almost lost her."

"Crazy, the way things turn out," John mused, his eyes on Odalie as she paused to speak to Maddie. "My sister, Attila the Hun, is ending up as Maddie's best friend. Go figure."

"I wouldn't have believed it myself. Odalie's quite a girl."

John smiled. "I thought it would be you and Odalie, eventually."

Cort shook his head. "We're too different. Neither of us would fit in the other's world. It took me a long time to realize that. But I saw my future in Maddie's eyes. I always will. I hope Odalie finds someone who can make her half as happy as I am today. She deserves it."

John nodded. "I'm very proud of her. She's matured a lot in the past few months." He turned back to Cort. "Christmas is next week. You guys coming home for it or not?"

"Oh, we have to . . . my folks would kill us, to say nothing of Sadie." He indicated the older woman in her pretty blue dress talking to some other people. "Maddie's like the daughter she never had. They can't have Christmas without us," he stated. "We're just going down to Panama City for a couple of days. Maybe later I can take Maddie to Europe and show her the sights. Right now, even a short plane trip is going to make her uncomfortable, much less a long one to somewhere exotic."

"I don't think Maddie will mind where you go, as long as she's with you," John said. "I wish you all the best. You know that."

"Thanks, bro."

"And when you come home, maybe we can crack open some new video games, now that my sister won't complain about my having you over," he added with a sigh.

Cort just grinned.

The hotel was right on the beach. It was cold in Panama City, but not so cold that they couldn't sit on the patio beyond the glass sliding doors and look at the cold moonlight on the ocean.

Predictably, they'd barely made it into the hotel room when all the months of pent-up anguished desire were taken off the bridle for the first time.

He tried to be gentle, he really did, but his

body was shivering with need long before he could do what he wanted to do: to show his love for Maddie.

Not that she noticed. She was with him every step of the way, even when the first encounter stung and made her cry out.

"This is part of it," he gritted, trying to slow down. "I'm so sorry!"

"Don't . . . sweat it," she panted, moving up to meet the furious downward motion of his hips. "You can hang out . . . the bedsheet in the morning . . . to prove I was a virgin . . . !"

"Wha-a-at?" he yelped, and burst out laughing even as his body shuddered with the beginning of ecstasy.

"First . . . base," she choked out, and bit him.

It was the most glorious high he'd ever experienced. He groaned and groaned as his body shuddered over hers. The pleasure was exquisite. He felt it in every cell of his body, with every beat of his heart. He could hear his own heart-beat, the passion was so violent.

Under him, her soft body was rising and falling like a pistol as she kept pace with his need, encouraged it, fanned the flames and, finally, glued itself to his in an absolute epiphany of satisfaction that convulsed both of them as they almost passed out from the climax.

She clung to him, shivering with pleasure in the aftermath. Neither of them could stop moving, savoring the dregs of passion until they drained the cup dry.

"Wow," she whispered as she looked into his eyes.

"Wow," he whispered back. He looked down their bodies to where they were joined. They hadn't even thought of turning out the lights. He was glad. Looking at her, like this, was a joy he hadn't expected.

"Beautiful," he breathed.

She smiled slowly. "And to think I was nervous about the first time," she said.

"Obviously unnecessary, since I have skills far beyond those of most mortal men . . . *oof!*"

She'd hit him. She grinned, though. And then she wiggled her eyebrows and moved her hips ever so slowly. Despite the sting, and the discomfort, pleasure welled up like water above a dam in a flood.

"Oh, yes," she whispered as he began to move, looking straight into her eyes. "Yes. Do that."

He smiled. "This," he murmured, "is going to be indescribable."

And it was.

When they got back, in time for the Christmas celebrations at Skylance, nobody could understand why, when Cort whispered, "first base," Maddie almost fell down laughing. But that was one secret neither one of them ever shared with another living soul.

About the Author

The prolific author of more than one hundred books, Diana Palmer got her start as a newspaper reporter. A multi-*New York Times* and *USA TODAY* bestselling author and one of the top ten romance writers in America, she has a gift for telling the most sensual tales with charm and humor. Diana lives with her family in Cornelia, Georgia.